DO OR DIE

"I've scouted for a lot of officers besides you. Captains, majors, colonels, even generals. Some of those generals are proud to call me a friend. What happens if I get word to them that you're the sorriest excuse for an officer I've ever met?"

"Are you threatening me?" Lieutenant Peter asked.

"I damn sure am. And the first one I'll get word to is General McCallister. He doesn't like jackasses any more than I do."

"McCallister?" Peters blanched.

"To save the girl and the lives of your men and your career, this is how we're going to do it." Fargo explained his plan.

"Sounds good to me, sir," Sergeant Rhodes commented when Fargo was done.

Lieutenant Peters had listened with his lips a thin slit and his eyes flashing with resentment. "It sounds feasible," he conceded. "And the important thing is the girl."

"There's hope for you yet," Fargo said.

"I just pray nothing goes wrong."

"You and me both," Fargo replied. "Because if it does, the buzzards will feast on us."

THE
TRAILSMAN
#359

PLATTE RIVER GAUNTLET

by

Jon Sharpe

A SIGNET BOOK

SIGNET
Published by New American Library, a division of
Penguin Group (USA) Inc., 375 Hudson Street,
New York, New York 10014, USA
Penguin Group (Canada), 90 Eglinton Avenue East, Suite 700, Toronto,
Ontario M4P 2Y3, Canada (a division of Pearson Penguin Canada Inc.)
Penguin Books Ltd., 80 Strand, London WC2R 0RL, England
Penguin Ireland, 25 St. Stephen's Green, Dublin 2,
Ireland (a division of Penguin Books Ltd.)
Penguin Group (Australia), 250 Camberwell Road, Camberwell, Victoria 3124,
Australia (a division of Pearson Australia Group Pty. Ltd.)
Penguin Books India Pvt. Ltd., 11 Community Centre, Panchsheel Park,
New Delhi - 110 017, India
Penguin Group (NZ), 67 Apollo Drive, Rosedale, Auckland 0632,
New Zealand (a division of Pearson New Zealand Ltd.)
Penguin Books (South Africa) (Pty.) Ltd., 24 Sturdee Avenue,
Rosebank, Johannesburg 2196, South Africa

Penguin Books Ltd., Registered Offices:
80 Strand, London WC2R 0RL, England

First published by Signet, an imprint of New American Library,
a division of Penguin Group (USA) Inc.

First Printing, September 2011
10 9 8 7 6 5 4 3 2 1

The first chapter of this book previously appeared in *Six-Gun Vendetta*, the three
hundred fifty-eighth volume in this series.

Copyright © Penguin Group (USA) Inc., 2011
All rights reserved

 REGISTERED TRADEMARK—MARCA REGISTRADA

Printed in the United States of America

The Trailsman

Beginnings . . . they bend the tree and they mark the man. Skye Fargo was born when he was eighteen. Terror was his midwife, vengeance his first cry. Killing spawned Skye Fargo, ruthless, cold-blooded murder. Out of the acrid smoke of gunpowder still hanging in the air, he rose, cried out a promise never forgotten.

The Trailsman they began to call him all across the West: searcher, scout, hunter, the man who could see where others only looked, his skills for hire but not his soul, the man who lived each day to the fullest, yet trailed each tomorrow. Skye Fargo, the Trailsman, the seeker who could take the wildness of a land and the wanting of a woman and make them his own.

*The sprawling prairie, 1861—where hostiles
and beasts drenched the grass with blood.*

1

They were eight days out of Camp Franklyn when they came on the slaughter.

Skye Fargo was half a mile ahead of the patrol. The day before he had come on the tracks of unshod horses and now the soldiers were pushing to overtake the Indians and find out if they were friendly or hostiles.

Fargo rode with his Henry across his saddle. He was a big man, broad at the shoulders, narrow at the hips. Buckskins clad his whipcord frame. Around his neck was a red bandanna and around his waist a gun belt and a Colt. His lake blue eyes constantly roved the ground and the horizon.

Dark specks in the sky to the east drew his interest, and brought a frown. He tapped his spurs to the Ovaro and the stallion broke into a trot. The specks grew and became circling buzzards.

The prairie rose to a grassy swell that hid whatever drew the carrion eaters.

Fargo slowed to a walk and drew rein when he was near the top. Dismounting, he dropped onto his belly and snaked high enough to see.

The homestead wasn't much to brag about. A simple soddy, with a sod corral. It didn't even have a door. Only a torn, faded piece of blanket for a curtain, flapping in the wind. A body lay a few feet from the shadowed doorway, another farther around.

"Hell," Fargo said. He saw no sign of the culprits and reckoned it was safe. Rising, he snagged the stallion's reins and walked down. Buzzards already on the ground took reluctant wing.

The homesteader had been chopped and sliced and hacked.

His wife had tried to reach the corral and their horse. She never made it.

Entering the soddy, Fargo nearly tripped over a third body. It was the daughter. She wasn't more than ten. He went back out and sat with his back to the wall.

Flies buzzed about the pools of blood; a big one was crawling in and out of what was left of the homesteader's nose.

"Jackass," Fargo said. The man had had no business bringing his family so far from anywhere. People back east couldn't seem to get it through their thick heads that the West wasn't tamed. Once they crossed the Mississippi River they left civilized life, with its laws and security, behind. Out here, the only law was be quick or be dead.

Plucking a stem of grass, Fargo stuck it in his mouth and settled back to wait. He heard the rumble of hooves and the clatter of accoutrements long before the patrol came over the swell.

Lieutenant Peters sat his saddle ramrod stiff. He looked too young to be an officer. Every night he polished his shoes and when on the move he constantly brushed dust from his uniform. Drawing rein, Peters gaped at the bodies and the flies. "My God."

"First you've ever seen?" Fargo was aware that this was the lieutenant's third patrol, ever.

"What?" Peters said absently, unable to tear his eyes from the hideous remains.

"Mutilated bodies," Fargo said.

"Oh, yes." Peters swallowed and wheeled his mount. "Sergeant Rhodes, form a burial detail. We will see to these good people and then go after the savages responsible."

Rhodes was a block of muscle, a veteran of the Indian campaigns. "Yes, sir," he dutifully responded. "If you're sure that's wise, sir."

Lieutenant Peters cocked his head. "How can it not be, Sergeant? We mustn't let the perpetrators go unpunished."

"If you say so, sir," Sergeant Rhodes said, swinging down. "But you might want to talk to our scout."

Peters turned to Fargo. "What does he mean, I should talk to you? I know Colonel Danvers instructed me to heed your advice but what can you possibly say that will change my mind?"

"There are twice as many hostiles as there are of us," Fargo said.

"Yes, you already told me that. But we can't let that deter us."

"We should," Fargo said.

Lieutenant Peters sniffed. "I wouldn't have taken you for a coward. You come highly recommended. The colonel says you're one of the best."

"Then maybe you should get your head out of your ass and listen."

Some of the troopers overheard and cracked grins.

"I beg your pardon," Peters said.

"You heard me," Fargo said. "We go after them, we're asking for a massacre."

"How very dramatic of you. I assure you my men can handle three times as many savages."

"No," Fargo said. "You can't. These are Lakotas. Or Sioux, as you probably call them. Miniconjous, I suspect. Most are seasoned warriors." He gestured at the column of soldiers on horseback. "Your men are almost all green recruits. Hell, most have peach fuzz on their chins."

"We are *soldiers*," Lieutenant Peters said archly. "Professionals, I might add. We can hold our own against a bunch of unorganized primitives. We have carbines, after all, and what do they have? Bows and arrows."

"God Almighty."

"What?"

"You're so full of yourself, it's a wonder you don't burst those shiny buttons." The officer colored with anger, and Fargo went on. "These primitives, as you call them, climbed on their first horse about the same time they learned to walk. They can ride rings around you. As for weapons, your men have Springfields. At best they can fire two or three shots a minute. A Sioux warrior can let eight arrows fly in the same time."

"Enough," Lieutenant Peters said. "Do you seriously intend to sit there and advise me not to pursue the renegades who committed these atrocities?"

"You sure like big words," Fargo said. "But yeah, if you know what's good for you, you won't."

"Your advice had been noted and rejected," Lieutenant Peters declared. "Now tell me. How far ahead would you say the hostiles are?"

"Not more than a couple of hours."

"Good. Mount up. We'll overtake them and make them pay."

"Or be wiped out," Fargo said.

2

They rode hard under a burning sun.

The tracks were plain enough that Lieutenant Peters could follow them without Fargo's help. Peters was so eager to have his revenge that he rode hunched forward in the saddle, his face practically glowing with bloodlust.

Fargo had fallen back and to one side of the troopers. He was angry that Peters had ignored his advice but it wasn't as if he hadn't seen it coming. Some people, Peters among them, had "jackass" branded on their foreheads in invisible letters.

Sergeant Rhodes detached from the column and brought his animal alongside the Ovaro. "What do we do?"

"Die, I reckon."

"I'm serious," Rhodes said. "How can I convince him this is the worst mistake he could make?"

"You could talk yourself blue in the face and it wouldn't do any damn good."

"There has to be something." Sergeant Rhodes motioned at the troopers, all of whom were ten to twenty years younger than he was. "I'm responsible for these boys."

"I have an idea," Fargo said. "We'll hit Peters over the head and tie him up and take him to Camp Franklyn."

"You're no help at all."

"What I am is the scout, and scouts can't tell officers what to do. Not even wet-nosed snots like Lieutenant Peters."

"It would help if you rode on ahead," Sergeant Rhodes said. "Warn us when we're getting close."

"Are you telling me or asking me?"

"One friend to another."

"Hell," Fargo said. He flicked his reins and caught up to Peters. "Lieutenant?"

5

The young officer didn't respond.

"The Sioux might spot our dust. I'd best make sure we don't ride into an ambush." Fargo brought the Ovaro to a trot. When he eventually glanced back, the troopers and their horses were moving sticks.

From then on Fargo went slow and careful. He'd lived with the Sioux. He knew how crafty they could be and he didn't care to be turned into a pincushion for their arrows.

Their trail led to the northeast over mile after mile of flat, broken now and again by a hillock or an occasional buffalo wallow. Twice Fargo spied antelope. He'd have tried to drop one for the soldier boys to eat but the sound could carry for a mile or more.

Along about two in the afternoon the prairie sprouted a legion of dirt mounds and dark holes; it was a prairie dog town. The sentries whistled in alarm and brown forms flew down their holes.

Fargo gave the town a wide berth. All it took was a single misstep to break a horse's leg.

A half hour more and a belt of woodland appeared. Cottonwoods, mostly, which told Fargo a stream was near. The war party could be, too.

Fargo reined to the south. The Sioux could be watching their back trail. When he had gone far enough he reined east again and presently came to a stop in the shade of tall oaks within sight of a gurgling blue ribbon. Sliding down, he wrapped the reins around a trunk, shucked the Henry from the saddle scabbard, and levered a round into the chamber.

A swallowtail butterfly flitted among purple flowers. Somewhere a frog croaked.

Fargo cat-footed north. He hoped he was mistaken and that the Sioux had pressed on. He figured they were likely in a hurry to reach their village and be with their families and friends. But the acrid smell of wood smoke disabused him of the notion. Crouching, he crept forward.

A bend in the stream provided a perfect spot to camp. The Sioux had grass for their horses, as well as water. A small fire crackled.

No doubt, Fargo imagined, some were off hunting game. He flattened. He considered running off their horses but several warriors stood guard. None of the faces was familiar, which was a relief. He hated to fight warriors he once called friends.

He debated walking on over and making their acquaintance. They wouldn't kill him outright. They'd be curious. Some might have heard of him. Maybe he could persuade them to ride on before the patrol got there.

Then some of the warriors clustered near the fire moved, and Fargo saw a white girl. She wasn't much over twenty. Her dress was torn and streaked with dirt. She sat with her knees tucked to her bosom and her arms around her legs, her face a study in misery. Whenever a warrior came anywhere near her, she looked up in fear.

The couple at the soddy must have been her parents, Fargo realized. She was lucky, in a way. One of the warriors had taken a shine to her and was taking her to his lodge.

This changed everything.

Until that moment Fargo had wanted to avoid a clash. Now there had to be one. Backing away, he rose and hurried to the Ovaro. He retraced his previous route and raced westward. The dust cloud the troopers raised made him inwardly cringe but they were far enough off that the Sioux hadn't spotted it.

Lieutenant Peters raised his arm to bring the detail to a halt. He wore a mocking smirk as he said, "Let me guess, scout. You rushed back to warn me yet again that there are too many hostiles and I should turn around before it's too late?"

"There are too many," Fargo said, "but you have to attack. There's more at stake than you being a jackass."

"Here now," Peters said.

"They have a girl."

"What?"

"You heard me. Probably the other daughter of that sodbuster. We have to get her away from them."

"For once we wholeheartedly agree." Lieutenant Peters smiled. "We'll hit them so hard and fast they won't stand a chance."

"No," Fargo said.

"What the hell do you mean, 'no'? I'm in charge. We do what I say and not what you say."

Fargo moved the Ovaro in so close, their legs brushed, and lowered his voice so only Peters and Sergeant Rhodes heard him. "Listen good, pup. That girl is in for hell unless we pull her out and I'm not about to let you ruin our chances."

"I won't be talked to like this."

"Yes, you will," Fargo said, "and I'll tell you why. I've scouted for a lot of officers besides you. Captains, majors, colonels, even generals. Some of those generals are proud to call me a friend. What happens if I get word to them that you're the sorriest excuse for an officer I've ever met?"

"Are you threatening me?"

"I damn sure am. And the first one I'll get word to is General McCallister. He doesn't like jackasses any more than I do."

"McCallister?" Peters blanched.

"To save the girl and the lives of your men and your career, this is how we're going to do it." Fargo explained his plan.

"Sounds good to me, sir," Sergeant Rhodes commented when Fargo was done.

Lieutenant Peters had listened with his lips a thin slit and his eyes flashing with resentment. "It sounds feasible," he conceded. "And the important thing is the girl."

"There's hope for you yet," Fargo said.

"I just pray nothing goes wrong."

"You and me both," Fargo replied. "Because if it does, the buzzards will feast on us."

3

Fargo figured the Sioux would stay put for the night and he was right.

The shadows were lengthening. Two small fires had been kindled and the warriors were relaxing. The girl was left alone except once when a young warrior took her a piece of deer meat.

He said something and poked her with his moccasin but she refused to take it. He took a bite himself and walked away.

Fargo marked the setting sun. By now the soldiers should have been in position. Their timing was crucial. If Peters waited too long the troopers might be wiped out.

A bugle note keened on the cooling air. The effect on the Sioux was to galvanize them into grabbing their weapons and leaping to their feet. They looked about in confusion until a sharp-eyed warrior pointed through the trees to the west and shouted, "Bluecoats!" There was a mad dash for their mounts. In the excitement everyone joined the rush; they forgot about the girl.

If Peters had done as Fargo told him, the soldiers were two hundred yards out on the prairie, their Springfields at the ready. When the war party crashed out of the trees, they would be met by a hailstorm of lead. It should break their charge and scatter them. It helped that the Sioux were riding into the sun and would have the glare in their eyes.

At a shout from a large warrior, the Sioux yipped and shrieked and poured toward their enemies.

Fargo started to rise, and froze.

A warrior had turned back. The same young one reined over to the girl and slid down. He didn't look happy about being left out of the battle. He stood with his back to her, staring after his friends.

Fargo moved quickly. In moments he was behind her unsuspecting captor and raised the Henry to bash him over the head.

The girl looked up. Amazement etched her grime-streaked face and she blurted, "Thank God!"

The young warrior whirled. He was armed with a lance and instantly attacked.

Fargo slammed the Henry against the shaft, seeking to knock the weapon from the young warrior's grasp but the Lakota held on and sprang back. Fargo could have shot him but the other Sioux would have heard. He sidestepped a second thrust and backpedaled, and when his young foe hurtled at him, he did the last thing anyone would expect; he threw the Henry at the man's face. The warrior ducked and Fargo was on him in a bound, driving his fist against the younger man's jaw. The blow rocked him. Fargo unleashed a left to the gut and a right cross that staggered him. An uppercut finally brought him down.

Fargo snatched up his Henry.

The rest of the war party was sweeping toward the troopers.

"Who are you?" the girl asked. "Where did you come from?"

Fargo couldn't believe she was still sitting there. "On your feet, damn it," he said, and grabbed her arm. "We have to get the hell out of here."

"I'm Mandolyn Brewster," she said as they ran. "Everyone calls me Mandy. Who might you be?"

"Not now," Fargo snapped. Introductions could wait. Staying alive was more important.

"Are you with the soldiers?"

Fargo skirted an oak.

Out on the prairie Lieutenant Peters bawled, "Fire!" and a volley thundered.

"Didn't you hear me?"

"Hush, girl." Fargo was concentrating on reaching the Ovaro. A distraction could prove fatal.

"What's the matter with you? I'm trying to be nice."

"Save it for later." Fargo avoided briars that would tear at her legs and went around a boulder. The stallion had its ears pricked. Fargo looked but saw no one.

Out on the prairie the din of battle raged.

Fargo swung up, shoved the Henry into the scabbard, and offered his hand. "Climb on."

Mandy reached up. Suddenly her eyes widened and she cried, "Look out!"

Drawing his Colt as he turned, Fargo twisted in his saddle. A warrior on horseback was bearing down on them and notching an arrow to a bowstring. Fargo fired from the hip, two swift shots that sent the Sioux tumbling. He saw no others and bent again, urging, "Hurry."

"My God, you're greased lightning," she said as she levered her leg up and over. "And you still haven't told me who you are."

"Call me Skye. Now hold on."

Fargo rode with the Colt in his hand. The plan called for him to spirit the girl to the west. The soldiers were to hold their ground for ten minutes, then retreat. He'd wait for them and they would escort the girl to Camp Franklyn.

They made it to the edge of the trees without being spotted. To the north the fight raged in blood-drenched earnest. Half a dozen warriors littered the grass. The rest circled the troopers, screeching and raising war whoops to the sky just out of range of the Springfields.

"The army came so quickly," Mandy said in his ear. "How did you know I'd been taken captive?"

"We didn't."

"It was awful. We were just sitting down to breakfast. Ma heard the horses act up and went outside to see why. We heard her scream and Pa ran out to help her but they stuck arrows in him and—"

"Not now," Fargo said yet again, and used his spurs. They were several hundred feet south of the Lakotas, and with any luck, the Sioux wouldn't spot them.

"Where are you going? Shouldn't we try to reach the soldiers?"

"Hold tighter," Fargo commanded. They were going at a gallop and her arm was holding him too loosely.

11

Mandy put her lips to his ear again. "How good is this horse of yours?"

"It's the best one I've ever had," Fargo boasted. "It can go forever if I need it to."

"You do," Mandy said, and pointed.

Five Sioux had broken from the rest and given chase.

4

Fargo had confidence in the Ovaro. Given a big enough lead the stallion could outdistance most any horse alive. But the Sioux possessed superb mounts too, and as riders they were second to none. The five had cut the distance in half before Mandy noticed them.

"They're gaining!" she hollered.

Fargo flew.

The Lakotas gave voice to fierce cries and pumped their lances and bows in the air.

Fargo couldn't let them get within arrow range; they were uncanny archers.

"They'll catch us," Mandy bawled.

Not if Fargo could help it. He resorted to his spurs again even though it wasn't necessary. The Ovaro was bearing double but still as fast as any of their pursuers.

The bugle blared. Fargo glanced back and saw the troopers forming in swift order. They were preparing to break out of the ring of Sioux. But it was too soon. They were supposed to wait longer.

An arrow whizzed out of the sky and sank inches deep into the earth.

Mandy dug her fingers into his side so hard it hurt. "That almost got us!"

One of the Lakotas had pulled ahead of his fellows and was nocking another arrow.

Fargo reined to the left and then the right, a zigzag pattern that should make them harder to hit. Another arrow fell behind them.

Suddenly a dry wash loomed. Fargo galloped down it and up the other side without the Ovaro breaking stride. On they fled, to the southwest. When an isolated stand of trees appeared, he reined toward them. As he drew near he recognized the trees as hackberries.

"Why are you slowing?" Mandy asked.

Fargo thought it should be obvious. He sprang down, grabbed the Henry, and took a bead before the Lakotas could guess his intent.

The bowman was out in front, raising the bow.

Fargo centered his sights and stroked the trigger. At the blast the archer tumbled. He took quick aim at another but the rest reined wide.

"You got one!" Mandy squealed.

Fargo hadn't realized she had come up behind him. Shoving her toward a tree, he barked, "Take cover."

The four Sioux were circling.

"This is a fine fix," Mandy said. "What if they hold us here until others come?"

"They're welcome to try." Fargo moved along the edge of the stand, keeping them in sight. He'd like to whittle the numbers down but they were too wary. He stepped into the open, thinking they might take the bait. They didn't.

Mandy had followed him. "We have to keep going, I tell you."

Tired of her carping, Fargo replied, "We will when I'm ready."

"Consarn it all, you'll get us killed."

"Go pester the Sioux, why don't you?"

"I do not intend to stay here until more of them show," she insisted.

Fargo didn't, either. From the bedlam back the way they had come, he needn't have worried. The boys in blue were keeping the war party busy. As for the four who had chased them, he was sorely tempted to bang off a shot although they weren't close enough. They continued to circle and he continued to keep track of them. The girl nervously trailed along.

"You're worried over nothing," he told her. "The rest of the Lakotas don't know we're here."

When Mandy didn't answer, Fargo turned.

She was gone.

Fargo wondered where she had got to. A whinny gave

him the answer. With an oath he broke into a run. Off through the hackberry trees he caught sight of Mandy trying to climb on the Ovaro. She had hold of the reins and had one hand on the saddle horn. The stallion was shying and snorting. "Let go of him, damn you!"

If she heard him, she wasn't about to.

Fargo ran faster.

Mandy lost her grip on the saddle horn and grabbed the Ovaro's mane. The stallion liked that even less. Rearing, it sent her tumbling.

Fargo was almost there. He was so intent on her antics that he failed to see a melon-sized rock. His boot came down on top of it and it slid out from under him and he crashed down hard on his elbows and knees.

Mandy renewed her attempt to mount. She snatched the reins again and managed to hook a foot in a stirrup. The Ovaro nickered and pranced. In desperation she flung herself at the saddle and wrapped both arms around the horn. For a few moments the stallion was still. Then without warning it bucked, its legs rigid, its back bent like a Sioux bow.

Mandy sprawled in the dirt.

By then Fargo was up and forced his legs to pump but he was too late.

The Ovaro had wheeled and was trotting off—toward the Lakotas.

5

Skye Fargo seldom struck a female. The few times he had, it was because the woman was trying to stick him with a knife or shoot him or, in the case of a paid assassin he had once tangled with, was kicking the tar out of him. But he came close to hitting Mandolyn Brewster. He stopped with his fist balled. "Damned idiot," he growled, and ran after the Ovaro.

"It was the horse's fault!" she hollered.

The four warriors had stopped and were watching the stallion approach, talking excitedly among themselves. To the Sioux, a good horse was worth its weight in buffalo hides. Some warriors valued their war horses so highly that when enemies were known to be in the vicinity of their village, they brought the horses into their lodge at night so they couldn't be stolen.

Fargo had seconds in which to do something. Leaning the Henry against his leg, he stuck his thumb and his first finger in his mouth, holding them slightly apart, the tips against his bottom teeth. Pressing his lips together, he flattened his tongue, sucked air into his lungs, and blew out.

The piercing whistle brought the Ovaro to a stop. As it had been trained to do, the stallion turned and came toward him.

One of the Sioux yipped and galloped to catch it.

Fargo jerked the Henry to his shoulder. He sighted and waited for the warrior to come within range.

The Sioux saw him take aim and reined away.

Trotting to the stand, the Ovaro stopped. Fargo patted its neck and spoke softly and led it into the trees.

Mandy was standing with her arms crossed and her expression dour. "You're mean. Do you know that?"

Fargo looped the reins around a low branch and faced

her. "Try to take my horse again and I'll break your damn arm."

"See?" Mandy said. "You have no call to treat me like this."

"Trying to run off like you did is plenty of reason. If you were a man, I'd have shot you."

"Honestly, now," Mandy said peevishly. "I think you're overreacting."

"And I think I should have left you with the Sioux." Which reminded Fargo. He jogged to the east side. There was no sign of more Sioux, which was good. There was no sign of the soldiers anywhere, either, which wasn't so good. He returned to the Ovaro and the girl. "We'll wait until dark and try to slip away."

"I think they have an idea of their own," Mandy said, gesturing.

The four Sioux were still to the south but they were separating. One headed east. Two others went to the west.

Fargo marked them as the first one circled until he was due east. The other two circled in the opposite direction. One drew rein when he was due west. The last went around the stand until he was to the north, and he too, stopped.

"They have us surrounded," Mandy stated the obvious. "What are they up to?"

The way Fargo saw it, either the warriors intended to keep them there until more showed up, or it was something more sinister. The grass was high enough that if they dismounted and snaked on their bellies, they could reach the hackberries without being seen. As if they had read his mind, each warrior dismounted. "Damn."

"They're coming for us, aren't they?"

"It's nice to know you're not completely stupid," Fargo said.

"Cut that out," Mandy said peevishly. "I'm sorry. All right? From now on I won't go near your horse without your say-so."

Fargo looked at her. Her face was dirty and her hair disheveled and her dress was a mess but she wasn't hard on the eyes. Her own were a nice green, and she had large breasts and legs that went on forever. "How old are you?"

17

"Why do you want to know?"

"Just answer the question."

"I'm nineteen. A grown woman, if you must know, and not a child, although that's how you treat me."

"Grown, huh?" Fargo said, and chuckled.

Mandy flushed. "I am so. I've been with a man, and everything."

"One man doesn't make you a woman."

"What do you know? You're not female. You don't know the first thing about what it's like."

"Girl, I've been with *real* women," Fargo said. "Women who have been with more men than you have fingers and toes."

"That's just like a man," Mandy said, "to judge women by how many men they've slept with. What about a woman who falls in love and marries and stays with just one man her whole life long? Does that make her less in your eyes?"

"Don't put words in my mouth," Fargo said. "The point is that you're hardly full grown."

Mandy put her hands on her hips. "I know some farm boys who think me an eyeful."

"You are at that," Fargo conceded. "But a person can be grown on the outside and only half grown inside."

"That is the silliest—" Mandy stopped. "Say, where did the Indians get to?"

Fargo glanced to the north, then the east, south, and west. The warhorses were there but the warriors weren't. They had gone to ground.

Unwrapping the Ovaro's reins, Fargo forked leather. "Up you go," he said, offering his hand.

"What are we doing?" Mandy asked as she settled behind him.

"Getting the hell out of here."

"Oh. I see. They made a mistake, didn't they, leaving their horses like that?"

"They figured we'd stay in the trees," Fargo said. "They figured wrong." He gigged the stallion to the west end of the stand, careful to stay in shadow. An idea occurred to him, and he grinned. "Can you ride bareback?"

"Are you kidding? I'm a farm girl. I never owned a saddle my whole life."

"You see that horse yonder?"

"Of course."

"If it doesn't run off when we get close, you're to hop down and jump on."

Mandy giggled. "We're going to steal one of their horses? That's marvelous. What are you waiting for? Let's go."

"The warrior who owns that animal is somewhere in the grass between us."

"He'll try to stop us, won't he?"

"He sure as hell will."

6

A prick of Fargo's spurs and the Ovaro shot out of the hackberry trees. He had his Colt in his right hand and when a bronzed figure rose with an arrow nocked to a sinew string, he banged off a swift shot. The warrior dropped and Fargo reined wide. He didn't take his eyes off the spot and it proved prudent. The Lakota reared again, the string pulled to his cheek, the barbed tip of the arrow glinting in the sunlight. Fargo fired again. Scarlet sprayed from the warrior's shoulder and he tottered.

They reached the horse, a pinto. Fargo thought it would run off but it stood there and let Mandy clamber on.

The wounded warrior was yelling for his friends to come to his aid.

"Stay close," Fargo shouted, and barreled westward.

For long minutes they flew across the prairie. When the pursuit he expected didn't appear, he slowed to spare their animals for later.

Mandy brought the pinto alongside. "That was mighty slick," she said, chuckling. "We got clean away."

No thanks to you, Fargo was tempted to say, but didn't. "Not yet we haven't."

"You reckon those others will come after us?"

"More than likely," Fargo said. It wasn't just that they'd stolen the pinto; they'd want Mandy back, too.

"We should find the troopers," she said. "We'll be safe with them."

"Why didn't I think of that?"

Mandy frowned. "I'm starting to think you don't like me much."

"You're a pain in the ass."

"I'm not trying to be," Mandy said, sounding hurt. "But you'll have to excuse me if I'm not in the best of moods. I lost my folks and my sis today, in case you've forgotten."

Fargo's conscience pricked him. He had, in fact, neglected to take that into account. "I'm sorry for you," he said to make amends. "This must be rough."

"It's awful," Mandy said, "and you're not helping matters by treating me like I'm a simpleton."

"You shouldn't have tried to take my horse."

"I thought we went through that? I'm sorry. All right? Sorry, sorry, sorry."

Now it was Fargo who chuckled. "What was that you said about being a grown woman?"

Mandy opened her mouth as if to give a sharp reply. She hesitated, her face softened, and she laughed. "I guess I deserve that. Maybe we should start over." She held out her hand. "I'm Mandolyn Brewster, and I'm very pleased to meet you."

To humor her, Fargo shook. "Likewise."

A doe and a fawn were grazing and watched them go by without a hint of fear. Butterflies flitted among the wildflowers. Overhead, cumulous clouds floated like fluffy forts.

"Moments like this," Mandy said softly, "are why I love the prairie."

Fargo had to hand it to her. She was holding up well, given the circumstances. "What will you do once you get to Camp Franklyn?"

Mandy shrugged. "I haven't thought that far ahead. All I could think of since the Sioux took me was about getting away. I haven't even had a chance to grieve for my parents."

Fargo imagined that when the damn broke, it would be a flood. "Hold it in a while longer if you can." The last thing he needed was for her to go to pieces.

"Can I ask you something?"

"I reckon you're entitled." Fargo supposed she wanted to know how far it was to Franklyn, or how soon they would hook up with the cavalry.

"Are you married?"

"Hell," Fargo said.

"Is that a yes or a no?"

"Am not, have never been, will never be."

Mandy arched an eyebrow. "That sounds so final. But a body never knows."

"I do."

"Are you one of those gypsies with a crystal ball? No one can predict what will be."

"I know me and I know how I like to live and a wife doesn't figure into it."

Fargo bore to the north. He reckoned a mile should be enough, and when they had gone that far and not cut the patrol's trail, he drew rein and scratched his chin in puzzlement.

"There's no sign of the soldiers, is there?"

"We'll wait here a spell. Could be they were delayed."

"Or wiped out."

Fargo preferred not to dwell on that. The colonel would blame him, and rightly so. He pushed his hat back on his head and squinted at the sun. "We have about four hours of daylight left."

"Then why wait? We can cover a lot of ground before nightfall."

"Looks like we don't have a choice," Fargo said, and extended an arm.

To the south the Sioux who had been after them were coming on fast.

7

The wide-open spaces of day were plunged in the pitch of a moonless night. A host of stars sparkled like gems, their pale light too feeble to illuminate much of anything.

Fargo rode with his hand on his Colt. Around them the wilds keened to the harsh yips of coyotes and the occasional wail of a roving wolf.

"Aren't you ever going to stop?" Mandy asked. "I can hardly keep my eyes open."

Small wonder, since by Fargo's reckoning, and the position of the Big Dipper, it was pushing midnight. "A few minutes more."

"God," Mandy said.

Fargo twisted in the saddle for the umpteenth time. He hadn't seen the Sioux since well before the sun went down. "We have to get far enough ahead that they won't sneak up on us in the middle of the night."

"I know. You've told me that five times now. But I'm still tired as can be."

From out of the dark came a growl.

"What was that?" Mandy asked in sudden fear.

"A farm girl can't tell a fox when she hears one?" Fargo said.

"I'd see a few now and then, sure, but it's not as if we had one for a pet. I had a cat named Chester." Mandy stopped.

Fargo recollected seeing it next to an overturned table in the soddy. By the size of the hole in its side, a warrior had driven a lance through its body. He changed the subject. "What I don't savvy is where those soldiers got to."

"They must have gone off and left you."

Fargo wouldn't put it past Lieutenant Peters but Sergeant Rhodes was cut from better cloth. Rhodes would never leave a man behind, and that included scouts.

"I wish we'd find a stream," Mandy said. "I could use a bath. A hot one would be wonderful but any water would do at this point."

"There's a stream about ten miles ahead," Fargo mentioned. They would reach it in the middle of the morning.

"That far? I can't stand feeling sweaty. Ever since I was little, my ma had me take three baths a week whether I needed them or not."

"A farm girl who can't stand sweat," Fargo said, and chuckled.

"Quit picking on me. Besides, we were sodbusters. My pa plowed and planted crops but we didn't have a farm. Not a real one with a barn and everything."

"You must have liked it."

"Why? Because I stayed with them as long as I did? That's not it at all. I love the prairie but I hated farming. We busted our backs from dawn till dusk six days a week plowing and planting and watering and harvesting and threshing. And when we weren't busy at farm work, we were cooking and sewing and mending. And what did it get us? Pa was always talking about how a few good years would have us sitting pretty but we were there five years and hardly ever had enough food to feed ourselves, let alone sell the extra."

"You didn't go off on your own because you like to starve?"

Mandy chortled. "You say the silliest things. I could have left anytime I wanted but I stuck with my folks because I loved them. And there was this boy."

"Ah," Fargo said.

"His name was Jasper. He lived about four miles north of us."

"Was?"

Mandy's voice dropped to a stricken tone. "He'd been courting me for about a year when one day he went off to hunt. His folks didn't think much of it when he wasn't home by dark. Sometimes when he shot a deer, he'd be late. But when ten o'clock came and went, they became worried.

They yelled their heads off but Jasper never answered. The next day his pa came to our place and asked my pa for help in finding him. I made the mistake of asking to go along."

"Mistake?"

"The Sioux had got hold of him. They did things—horrible things, things I wish I'd never seen. Some nights I can't sleep for the memory of it."

"No one deserves to die like that." Unfortunately, Fargo knew of a great many who had.

"They scooped out his eyes and stuck his eyeballs on sticks," Mandy related. "His tongue was gone. So was his left ear. I had to force myself to kneel down beside him and take his hand."

"There's no need to tell me this."

"It's important you understand. When I said a while back that I'm a grown woman, you didn't take me seriously."

"I won't make that mistake again," Fargo promised.

"I am grown in more ways than you can imagine," Mandy declared.

Fargo wondered if she was saying what he thought she was saying. He put it from his mind for the time being and drew rein. "This is far enough. We'll rest here for the night."

Mandy stared off every which way. "Out in the open like this? Are you trying to get us killed?"

"We can see for miles," Fargo explained. "And we can spot a fire from a long ways off."

"There's no protection from anything."

"Yes, there is," Fargo said, and patted his Colt.

They climbed down. Fargo untied his bedroll and spread out his blankets. He placed his saddle as a pillow, and motioned. "Your bed awaits."

"What about you?" Mandy asked. "Where will you sleep?"

"I'll stand guard." Fargo shucked the Henry from the saddle scabbard and went a few yards and sat facing east. If the Sioux were still coming, that was the direction they would come from.

"It's not fair to you." Mandy sank onto the blanket and leaned back against his saddle. "I have a better idea."

"Oh?"

Mandy patted the blanket. "Right here is as good a place as any. Come lie next to me."

"You might not be able to control yourself," Fargo joked.

Mandy's teeth were white in the darkness. "I don't intend to."

8

A long time ago Skye Fargo had come to two decisions. The first was to never try to understand women. They were unpredictable as hell. The second was to never say no to a lady who was willing. When it came to *that*, he'd be the first to admit he was like a buck in rut.

So now, after Mandy patted the blanket, Fargo went over and sat beside her. "You're a bundle of surprises," he said by way of sweet talk.

"Am I?" Mandy responded, and leaned against him. "It's been a terrible, tiring day. Can you blame me for wanting to relax and forget for a while?"

Fargo didn't blame her at all but he did wonder how she could suggest what she was suggesting so soon after her parents had been butchered. "We all have things we'd like to forget," he said to encourage her.

Mandy placed her cheek on his shoulder and gazed at the canopy of stars. "Jasper and me did it a lot. He'd sneak over at night. My folks always went to bed early and after they fell asleep I'd slip out and we'd, well, you know."

"I'm shocked."

Mandy laughed. "My folks would have been. My pa would have shot him and my ma wouldn't have spoke to me for a month of Sundays. She always warned me that a lady never sleeps with a man before the I do's. She'd say that all men are only after one thing, and why would they buy the cow when they get the milk for free?"

"Your mother was right."

"Jasper was willing to take me for his wife. He was getting up the nerve to ask my pa for my hand when he was killed." Mandy closed her eyes and bowed her head. "I thought that was the worst day of my life. Little did I know there could be even worse."

Fargo put an arm around her and pecked her on the head. To keep her in the mood he said, "A pretty girl like you, there will be other men who want to buy the cow. Whether you give milk is up to you."

"Moo," Mandy said, and looked at him and grinned. "Has anyone ever told you how good-looking you are?"

"Not today."

Mandy kissed his cheek. "I mean it. Jasper was good-looking but you beat him all hollow."

"This is how I popped out of the womb."

"You were born with a beard?" Mandy said, and laughed. "You're not at all like I expected a scout to be."

"How is that?"

"Oh, I don't know. You're not always chewing on tobacco and spitting and you don't curse a whole lot and you sure don't smell like the hind end of a buffalo."

"You've stuck your nose up a buff's ass?"

Mandy threw back her head and cackled. "Lordy, the things you say. But I mean it. You've treated me decent even though I've been a bit of a bitch."

"A bit?"

Mandy playfully punched him on the shoulder. "All right. I admit it. More than a bit. But I had cause."

Fargo was about to say that yes, she did, but he steered away from another mood spoiler. "What you need is a back rub. Lie down on your belly and I'll give you one."

"Oh, I love back rubs." Mandy turned over and lay flat, her chin on her crossed forearms. "I made Jasper give them to me all the time."

Fargo shifted, put his hands on her shoulders, and massaged in small circles.

"Goodness, that feels nice," Mandy cooed. "You can do that all night if you want."

Fargo had other things in mind.

"Can I ask you a question?"

"You're letting me touch your body. You can ask me damn near anything."

"This is serious. I don't have any kin that I'm close to. Pa lost his family when he was a boy and Ma's folks are living up in Canada somewhere."

"You want me to find them for you?"

"No. I aim to make it on my own." Mandy turned her head so she could see him. "But I don't know how to go about it. I mean, farming is pretty much all I know. What kind of work is there for women? And where's best for me to go?"

Fargo had met a lot of ladies who complained that there were far fewer opportunities for women than there were for men. A man could be just about anything but for women there weren't many jobs available. Most women didn't think that was fair. The truth be told, neither did he. "Can you sew?"

"Not very good. Ma tried to teach me but I'm all thumbs."

"Can you cook?"

"Halfway decent, I suppose," Mandy said. "But I wouldn't want to do it for a living. Sweat over a hot stove all day? No, thank you."

Fargo racked his brain. A seamstress and a cook were two jobs women could get fairly easy. Others were harder to come by. "There's always saloon work," he said, and felt her body tense under his hands.

"Wear a tight dress and let drunks grope me and maybe have to take them into a back room? I'd hate that."

"I don't know what else to suggest," Fargo admitted.

"Well, if you think of something, let me know. I'm not so prideful that I won't admit when I need help."

Fargo was massaging around her shoulder blades. He was surprised when she suddenly rolled over and his hands were on her breasts.

"Now, then," Mandy said, "suppose we stop flapping our gums and help each other relax?"

9

Fargo liked women who were direct. He didn't like women who played with men as if the men were puppets, the ones who made the man practically beg for it. He didn't like the teasers and the users. He ran into a lot of those. But a woman who was honest about her feelings, that was his kind of gal.

Bending, Fargo kissed Mandy on the mouth. She responded with fierce passion, kissing him so hard, she mashed her lips into his. Drawing back, he said, "What are you trying to do? Break my face?"

"Sorry," she said sheepishly. "I just want it, is all. I want to forget for a while. Help me, Skye. Help me forget this terrible day."

"I'll do what I can, ma'am," Fargo promised.

Their next kiss was better. She didn't try to pulp his mouth. When he ran his tongue along her lips, she parted them and her tongue slid out. Hers and his did a silken moist dance that sent a tingle down to his toes.

Fargo's hands were busy, too. He kneaded and sculpted her twin melons and felt her nipples harden under her dress. He began to undo her buttons with one hand while running his other down over her flat tummy to the junction of her thighs and then down one leg and up again and down the other. She squirmed, sparking his pole to iron hardness.

Around them coyotes raised their cries to the stars and an owl hooted but otherwise the night was peaceful.

Mandy didn't have a lot on under the dress. Farm girls usually didn't have the money for the petticoats and lacy chemises their city sisters wore. Mandy had a simple plain cotton shift that went from her neck to her knees. Underneath was bare skin.

Fargo took his sweet time. He ran his hands over every square inch of her luscious body. Her inner thighs deserved special attention. Some men liked a woman's breasts the most and some were leg men but for Fargo the soft sheen of an inner thigh was as close to perfect as life got except for the mount of Venus itself.

Mandy wasn't idle. Her hands explored him everywhere, and she wasn't always gentle about it. She liked it a little rough.

Once she pinched him so hard, he grunted. Another time, she cupped him, down low, and he thought she was going to rip them off.

Their bodies grew hot and their kisses became molten. When at long last Fargo parted her legs and placed his hand between them, she was wet and wanting. He parted her slit and rubbed her clit and the urgency of her need caused her to arch up into him.

"Yes," Mandy panted. "Oh, yes."

Fargo plunged his finger into her and had a bucking bronco on his hands. She grounded her mount into his palm as if she needed to start a fire with the friction. He inserted a second finger and she gasped and stopped moving.

"Oh," she said.

An earthquake took place under him. She gushed and fastened her teeth in his shoulder. When at length she subsided, she lay limp and caked with sweat and smiling.

"That was nice."

"We're just getting started."

Fargo built up to it. By the time he got around to kneeling between her legs, she was so desperate to be filled that she took hold of him and impaled herself with a deft dip of her hips.

"God in heaven," Mandy breathed. "I needed this so much."

"Don't we all?" Fargo said, which wasn't entirely true. He'd met women who were as cold as glaciers and had no interest in making love; he'd often wondered if there was something wrong with them. And he'd heard of men who were the same way.

Afterward, they lay side by side on their backs, her hand on his arm, her fingers lightly caressing.

"Thank you, kind sir."

"Anytime," Fargo said.

"I'll take you up on that." Mandy giggled. "Maybe it's best we never found the soldiers. I couldn't do it with all of them around."

"They'll give you a room at Camp Franklyn until you get around to deciding where you want to go."

"How long will you be there?"

"Soon as we get you there, I'm lighting a shuck." Fargo had agreed to scout for the patrol only as a favor to Colonel Danvers.

"I'd like to go with you."

Fargo looked at her. Some women thought that sleeping with a man was the same as owning him. He hadn't taken her for one of those. "I told you I'm not looking for a wife."

"That works out nice since I'm not looking for a husband. I just don't have anywhere else to go." Mandy kissed him on the shoulder. "What do you say? I promise not to be a burden."

"I'll think about it."

"Think about this," Mandy said, and grinning, she bit him where she had just kissed him. "You get to have me anytime you want. No strings attached."

"Damn," Fargo said.

10

Word was that Camp Franklyn would soon be torn down and moved. The army had a history of picking a site for a fort or long-term camp and then later discovering it wasn't suitable. In Franklyn's case, the First Colorado Cavalry had established it on lowland near the South Platte River. The site was fine if you loved mosquitoes and snakes and sweltering in the summer.

The camp was there to safeguard the settlers flocking to the region and to protect the Overland Trail.

Colonel Danvers had troopers clear out a room for Mandy Brewster and clean it from ceiling to floor.

The patrol had made it back days before Fargo and the girl. They only lost five troopers.

Colonel Danvers had commended Lieutenant Peters for his conduct and put him up for promotion, and Peters was strutting around like a peacock. Fargo didn't bother telling Danvers the truth.

Either Peters would grow up or one day an arrow or a lance would put an end to his airs.

Sergeant Rhodes was genuinely glad Fargo and the girl made it back safely. That first night, they sat at a fire passing a bottle back and forth.

Rhodes took a swig and let out a contented sigh. "Funny thing."

"What is?" Fargo asked. He was thinking about Mandy. She was to leave her window open so he could sneak into her room about midnight.

"It took you and Miss Brewster eleven days to get here."

"So?"

"So I could have gotten her here in five or six if I'd pushed it."

"She'd just lost her folks and been abducted by the Sioux," Fargo reminded him. "She wasn't in any shape for a lot of hard riding."

"She sure recovered fast. I've noticed how she smiles and hums a lot."

"Does she?"

"Especially when she's around you." Rhodes passed the bottle back.

"We're friends," Fargo said, and sipped.

"No fooling? I figured—" Rhodes abruptly stopped and shot to his feet. "Colonel Danvers, sir."

Fargo had heard someone coming toward them but hadn't realized it was the commanding officer.

"At ease, Sergeant," Danvers said. He had gray at the temples and was thickening around the middle from all the desk work he had to do. "Is that a bottle I see?"

"I'm off duty, sir," Rhodes said.

"I told you, at ease." Colonel Danvers held out his hand. "I wouldn't mind a drink myself."

Fargo passed the bottle. "Remember that time at Leavenworth when we had that drinking contest?"

"Do I ever." Danvers shook his head in amusement. "I thought I could handle my liquor but you drank me under the table." He looked at Rhodes. "This man drinks whiskey like it's water, Sergeant. We went through three bottles and he didn't even slur his words."

"He drank me into a stupor once, too, sir," Rhodes revealed.

Colonel Danvers wiped the mouth of the bottle on his sleeve and took a long swallow. He gave the bottle back and sat down.

"I owe you an apology."

"Me?" Fargo said.

Danvers nodded. "When you showed up this afternoon I forgot to give you something. My only excuse is that I was busy seeing to Miss Brewster's needs and to writing a report on her safe arrival." He reached into his jacket and pulled out a folded sheet of paper. "This came for you the day after you left on patrol. From what I can gather, he's sent a copy to every fort and camp on the frontier. It must be important for him to go to so much trouble."

Fargo opened it. The message was short and to the point. He read it out loud. "'Skye. Need your help. Meet me where I saved your life. Come quick. Great things in the works. Texas Jack.'"

"Texas Jack?" Sergeant Rhodes repeated. "Why do I feel I should know that name?"

"He's worked as a scout," Colonel Danvers said, "and he's almost as famous as our friend, here. If you'd met him, you would remember. Texas Jack is"—Danvers seemed to search for the right word—"colorful."

"What's his last name?"

"Lavender," Colonel Danvers said.

"Texas Jack Lavender?" Sergeant Rhodes said, and laughed.

"Don't ever do that to his face," Danvers advised. "He hates his last name worse than anything."

"Does he ever," Fargo said. In his mind's eye he saw the saloon they had been in one night when a drunken mule skinner saw fit to bait Texas Jack about it. The mule skinner mentioned as how it was a name more fit for a woman than for a man. Jack had smiled and got up and walked over and punched the mule skinner in the face. Unfortunately, the mule skinner outweighed Jack by about seventy pounds and had several friends. They pounced, and the unfair odds spurred Fargo into lending a hand. One of the mule skinners nearly busted his jaw. He could barely chew food for a week.

"This Jack is from Texas, I take it?" Sergeant Rhodes was saying.

"He's from Ohio," Fargo said. "Born and bred there. He ran away from home when he was twelve and has been on his own ever since."

"How did he get the name Texas Jack?"

"Jack lived there for a spell. Liked it so much, he added it to his name."

"I'll be damned," Rhodes said.

"What was that about him saving your life?" Colonel Danvers asked.

"It was about a year ago," Fargo related. "A grizzly almost got me." He relived it in his head; they had been hunting buffalo near where the Loup and Cedar rivers feed into the Platte, and they shot a bull but it didn't go down. It ran into the woods along the river and they followed it in and finished it off. He'd dismounted and set his rifle down and was on his knees, about to commence the skinning, when a grizzly charged out of the undergrowth. He had no time to grab his rifle or run. As if it were happening again he saw the bear's huge head bristling with savagery, saw those massive jaws gape wide to crush and rend. He'd looked death in its literal face—and was spared. Texas Jack put a slug from his Sharps into the grizzly's brainpan and the bear slid to a stop with its nose an inch from his leg.

Fargo realized Colonel Danvers was saying something.

"—must be a good friend of yours if he expects you to drop everything and go running."

"A man saves my hide, I figure I owe him," Fargo said. "Even if Jack does get me into trouble every time I turn around."

"Any idea what he wants?"

"With Jack there's no telling." Fargo still remembered the time Jack bet him that he could sneak up on an old elk cow and climb on and ride her. He'd lost twenty dollars on a stunt no sane person would attempt.

"When will you be leaving?"

"In the morning," Fargo decided. It would take ten to twelve days to get there. He could follow the Platte the entire way.

"That's too bad," Colonel Danvers said. "I was hoping you'd stick around awhile."

Sergeant Rhodes was taking a turn at the bottle. He smacked his lips and said, "Think your friend will get you into more trouble?"

"I sure as hell hope not," Fargo said.

11

From a distance it looked like a small army was assembled. A long row of tents had been set up a stone's toss from the Platte River. A rope corral had been rigged and twenty to thirty horses milled about. Dozens of men were engaged in a variety of tasks, most of them busy erecting a large fence that covered two to three acres. Several wagons were parked off under the trees.

"My word!" Mandy exclaimed. "You never mentioned anything like this."

Fargo was as flabbergasted as she was. "I thought there would just be Jack."

They had drawn rein on a small rise and the people below hadn't spotted them yet.

"What in the world can your friend be up to?"

"Maybe he's building a settlement so he can name it after himself," Fargo said, only half in jest.

"From what you've told me, this Texas Jack is quite a character." Mandy sat straighter and fluffed her hair. "How do I look?"

"Tossing me over for him?" Fargo said.

"Don't be silly. I haven't even met him. It's you I like at the moment."

Fact was, Fargo enjoyed her company, too. She didn't talk him to death like some women would, or preen all the time like some did, or demand he treat her special as certain ladies were wont to do. She didn't complain about helping to skin game and cook their supper. And at night she made love like a wildcat. "You're as fine a female as I've ever met," he admitted.

Mandy beamed with delight. "That's good to hear. I've tried awful hard to please you."

"Don't get too attached."

"I know. You've warned me that sooner or later you'll have to go your way and I'll have to go mine."

Fargo clucked to the Ovaro and they started down.

"What is that?" Mandy asked, and pointed beyond the fence.

At first Fargo thought it was a buffalo. Then he realized it was a contraption built to look *like* a buffalo; a buff hide with the head and horns attached had been thrown over a wooden frame. Several men on horseback were taking turns galloping past and throwing a rope at it.

"I've never seen the like," Mandy said.

Neither had Fargo.

Women were scarce on the frontier and Mandy created quite a stir. The men working on the fence stopped to stare. So did a lot of others.

"It's good I don't blush easy," she remarked.

Fargo made for a tent twice the size of the rest. The flap was tied open and someone was moving around inside. He had a hunch who it was and he was proven right when a man barreled out and jabbed a finger at the men by the fence.

"Why in hell did you stop working? I need that done two days from now, not next year."

Mandy drew rein and blurted, "My word. Is that your friend?"

"The one and only," Fargo confirmed.

Texas Jack Lavender was a strapping figure of a frontiersman. His shoulders were as broad as Fargo's, his frame almost as muscled. He also wore buckskins, but any resemblance between Fargo's and his was pure coincidence. Jack's whangs were twice as long and hung as thick as the leaves on a willow.

Blue and green beads lavishly decorated both his shirt and his pants. His belt boasted a silver buckle roughly the size of Connecticut and had silver conchos as big as hen's eggs. A bright yellow handkerchief was tied around his throat. On each hip, worn butt forward, was an ivory-handled Remington. His black leather boots had silver trim on the toes and the heels. But for all that, it was his hat that first drew the eye.

Custom-made for him by a hatmaker in Saint Louis, the crown was nearly a foot and a half high and the brim eight inches wide. Were it not for a strap tucked under his chin, the wind would whip it off. A wide silver band encircled it and engraved on the band in large letters was TEXAS JACK. He was holding a flask that he raised to his lips and chugged.

"It's been a spell, pard," Fargo said.

Texas Jack turned. A smile lit face and he lowered the flask. "Skye! You got my message, thank God!"

Fargo climbed down. His feet had barely touched the ground when Jack's arms were around him and he was spun in a circle, Jack whooping with delight.

"I was beginning to think you wouldn't show. And I need you, hoss. I need you more than anything."

Fargo clapped Jack on the back. "It's good to see you again, too." He motioned at the fence and the contraption with the hide. "But what is it you need me for?"

"Oh, you'll love this. I've had the brainstorm of all brainstorms." Texas Jack beamed. "I need you to help me catch a passel of buffalo and put them in that pen yonder."

"What?" Fargo wasn't sure he had heard right.

"And we should try not to get killed doing it."

12

Mandy was mesmerized. When Texas Jack took her hand and offered to help her down, she just sat there.

"Didn't you hear me, fair creature? Permit me to be of assistance." Jack shoved the flask at Fargo. Reaching up, he slid his hands under Mandy's arms and swung her from the saddle. He removed his hat, bowed with a flourish, and kissed the back of her hand. "Texas Jack, madam. Consider me your doting servant."

"Oh my," Mandy said.

"You have to watch him," Fargo advised. "His tongue is golden and his hands are everywhere."

Texas Jack frowned. "Slander, sir. A rumor started by that cute little muffin in Denver who couldn't get enough of me."

"I was there," Fargo reminded him, "and she didn't mean it as a compliment."

Texas Jack turned back to Mandy. "Pay him no mind, my dear. Although I like his company he has the breeding of a goat."

Mandy giggled. "He does not. I know him quite well by now and he's a perfect gentleman."

"Are we talking about the same cad?" Texas Jack asked. He looked from Fargo to her and back again. "And while we're at it, how is it that you show up with this beauty at your side?"

"She's a friend," Fargo said.

"A good friend," Mandy amended.

Texas Jack took a step back. "Do my eyes and ears deceive me? Can it be that at long last—?"

"What on earth are you babbling about?" Mandy said.

"My dear beauty," Texas Jack replied. "This man and I are like brothers. I know him better than I know anyone. Never, ever have I seen him in the company of a female unless it was in a saloon or a bawdy house." Jack studied her. "What makes you so special?"

"He saved me from the Sioux," Mandy said.

"That hardly explains it. He is forever rescuing damsels in distress." Tapping his chin, Texas Jack walked around her. "Hmmmmm. There's no denying you're lovely but I'd have thought he'd go for someone of a more earthy nature rather than apple pie."

"I beg your pardon."

"Jack," Fargo said.

"She is what she is," Jack said. Taking the flask, he upended it. His Adam's apple bobbed and he lowered the flask and licked his lips.

"You sure like to drink," Mandy said.

"The ambrosia of the gods," Texas Jack declared. "A nectar as sweet as honey."

"How you talk," Mandy said.

"'Tis a gift, my dear. I was born gabbing." Texas Jack motioned at the large tent. "After you. I imagine Skye is bursting at the seams to learn more of why I sent for him."

"I am curious," Fargo admitted.

The tent was made up like a room at the finest hotel. Rugs were spread over the ground. The bed was a four-poster with a flowered canopy. There was a table and three chairs and two large chests with padlocks.

Mandy went to the bed and touched the canopy. "I've only ever heard of beds this fancy. You must be rich."

"Alas, no, but I seek to remedy that." Texas Jack held out a chair for her. Once she sat, he claimed one for himself and patted the last. "Come on, hoss. I'm busting at the seams, too."

Fargo turned the chair and straddled it. "This better not be another of your loco schemes."

Texas Jack put a hand to his chest as if stricken. "When have I ever suggested anything half crazy?"

"There was that time you wanted to paint bricks yellow and sell them as gold bars."

"He didn't," Mandy said.

"Or that time down at the border when you wanted to set up a rooster farm."

"That would have worked. The Mexicans love their cock fights."

"Except you don't know the first damn thing about raising roosters."

"How hard can it be? You get a lot of chickens and have them lay a lot of eggs." Texas Jack sat back. "That's our problem right there. I come up with great ideas and you nitpick them to death."

"I know I'll regret this," Fargo said, "but let me hear your latest."

"To start we need buffalo."

Mandy laughed. "Whatever for? To try and catch them is plumb ridiculous. In the first place, you can't catch them like they are cows. And in the second place, what would you do with them once you've caught them? Sell them for meat?"

"I'll get to that in a moment." Texas Jack stood and began to pace, gesturing excitedly. "I was in Saint Louis a while ago and some Pawnees were there. Hiburu was with them. You know who he is, Skye."

Fargo nodded. Old Hiburu was a chief who had visited Washington and Philadelphia a few years ago.

"They caused quite a sensation," Texas Jack related. "Folks came from all over. And do you know why?"

"It wasn't that they were Indians," Fargo said. For years the Superintendent of Indian Affairs had had his office in Saint Louis, and a lot of Indians paid him a visit.

"No, it was what Hiburu was wearing," Texas Jack said. "A moth-eaten buffalo headdress, with the horns and all. People wanted to see it, to touch it."

"A headdress?" Mandy said.

"A lot of the people in Saint Louis are from back east, girl. They don't have buffalo back there. They don't have a lot of things that we have out here." Texas Jack placed both hands on the table. "The fuss they were making got me to thinking."

"Uh-oh," Fargo said.

"I'm serious, damn it," Texas Jack said. "It struck me that Hiburu could have charged for them to touch the damn thing and they'd have paid."

"So?" Fargo said.

Texas Jack raised his face to the top of the tent and addressed it as if he were addressing the Almighty. "Grant me patience. I have vision and the rest of the world wears blinders."

Mandy looked at Fargo. "Is your friend always so dramatic?"

"You haven't seen anything."

Texas Jack drew himself up to his full height. "This time I am on to something. Something great. Something grand. Something that can make us rich."

"I said it before and I'll say it again," Fargo said. "Uh-oh."

"Listen. If the folks in Saint Louis were that excited over a head and a hide, think how excited they'd be over the real article."

Mandy gasped. "You intend to take a buffalo all the way to Saint Louis?"

"Not *a* buffalo, pretty lady," Texas Jack said, "but a whole herd. Not only that, we'll take along some Indians and put on a show that will draw in crowds from all over. At a dollar a head we'll make money hand over fist."

"But how will you get the buffalo there?" Mandy questioned. "Buffalo are wild and dangerous."

"Have you ever heard of a bronc buster, sweet one?"

"Can't say as I have, no."

"That's what Texicans call a saddle stiff who makes his living breaking wild horses, and what's good enough for them is good enough for us." Texas Jack paused. "What we need is our very own buffalo buster." He grinned at Fargo.

"Oh, hell," Fargo said.

13

"No," Fargo said for the tenth time. "No. No. No. And, god-damn it, no."

They were out by the fence that was being built. The men working on it kept stealing glances at Mandy. One man stole his glance at the wrong moment; he hit his thumb with his hammer and cussed a livid streak.

"Here now," Texas Jack said, shaking his silver flask at him. "I won't have that kind of talk in the presence of a lady. One more cuss word, you thoughtless son of a bitch, and I'll by God fire your inconsiderate ass."

The man stopped cursing and glared at Jack.

Mandy said quietly, "You didn't have to do that on my account. My pa used to swear now and then. I'm used to it."

"Nonsense, my dear," Jack said with another of his gallant bows. "Chivalry isn't dead so long as I breathe."

"Oh brother," Fargo said.

"Scoff, sir," Texas Jack said, and swallowed more bug juice. "But I am a firm believer in always treating a lady *as* a lady. If I learned nothing else from *Ivanhoe*, I learned that."

"What is that?" Mandy asked.

"*Ivanhoe?* Why, it's only one of the greatest books ever written."

"You can read?" Mandy said.

Texas Jack drew himself up to his full height and placed his hand on his chest. "As a fish breathes water, so do I breathe the written word."

"I need a drink," Fargo said.

"My mother, bless her soul, taught me at an early age,"

Texas Jack went on. "I was barely out of the cradle when she placed my first book in my little hands."

"Really?"

"As God is my witness. I have been reading ever since. This uncouth lout next to you may scoff, but keep in mind he's never read a book in his life. He's more fond of liquor than he is of books."

Both Fargo and Mandy stared at the flask in Texas Jack's hand.

Jack coughed and wagged it. "Yes, well, I confess to a certain fondness for hard spirits myself. It's my nature to be passionate about things." He took her hand and kissed it again. "I am a fountain of passion."

"I think I'm going to be sick," Fargo said.

Texas Jack turned to the fence. "But back to the matter at hand. As you can see, once this is done it will easily hold a small herd of buffalo. Then all we have to do is tame them and off to Saint Louis we go."

"Tame *buffalo*?" Fargo said.

"Why not? What are they but shaggy cattle? I grant you they weigh more and they don't have the cheeriest of dispositions, but we can overcome that."

"You lunkhead. They won't let us get close enough to catch them."

"Ah," Texas Jack said, and smiled benignly. "I'm one ahead of you, sirrah."

"Sirrah?" Mandy said.

"We don't want to know," Fargo said.

Texas Jack led them toward the contraption with the buffalo hide draped over it. A man on horseback was racing toward it and whirling a rope. At the right moment he let the rope fly and the loop settled over the horns and the head.

"Did you see?" Texas Jack gloated. "That's how we'll do it. We'll swoop down on them and rope five or six and bring them here to tame them."

"You're an idiot," Fargo said.

"I don't know," Mandy said. "It might work."

"See?" Texas Jack said. "She appreciates genius when she hears it."

"Is genius brown?" Fargo retorted, and gestured at the contraption. "That thing isn't a real buff. It just sits there. A real buff will attack any jackass who tries to rope it, or if the jackass is lucky it will run off."

Texas Jack grinned. "That's why we have fast horses."

"You're hopeless," Fargo said.

"Skye, Skye, Skye," Texas Jack said, and put his arm on Fargo's shoulders. "How long have we been pards? Have I ever in all that time given you cause to doubt me?"

"I've lost count of your harebrained ideas."

"This one will work. And it will make us rich. Think of it! Think of all the money."

"Provided we don't get a buff horn in the gut." Fargo faced him. "Stand still."

"What?"

"You're so drunk, you're swaying. Let me see you stand perfectly still."

"What would that prove?"

"Jack, I'm not going to help you catch any buffalo and I'm sure as hell not going to try and tame them for you."

"Very well," Texas Jack said indignantly. "Then I'll do it myself." He tilted his face to the sky and raised an arm aloft. "Never let it be said that Texas Jack shirks his responsibilities. When there is a fray to leap into, I leap first. When there is a hurdle to jump over, I jump first."

"Isn't he wonderful?" Mandy said.

"I really need that drink," Fargo said.

14

Fargo didn't like tents. He preferred stars over his head to canvas. But Texas Jack offered them a tent of their own and Mandy practically begged him to accept.

It was near midnight. They'd spent hours listening to Jack prattle on about the riches to be had if only Fargo would go along with his grand design, as Jack called it.

"I've already got a name for it," Texas Jack mentioned at one point. "We'll call it the Great Frontier Extravaganza Starring Real Scouts of the Plains Complete with Raging Buffalo and Red Devils."

"Are you sure that's long enough?" Fargo said.

"Why not call it something simple?" Mandy suggested. "Something like a Wild West Show?"

Texas Jack shook his head. "That won't do, girl. We need a name that grabs the public's attention and interest. The Wild West is too dull."

"How about the Wild, Wild West?"

"Oh, please. That's even sillier."

Now, lying on his cot with a hand under his head and his boots still on, Fargo stared at the canvas and sighed. "I'm leaving in the morning," he announced.

Mandy was sitting on the other cot, prying at her buttons. She stopped prying. "You're going to run out on your friend? Poor Jack will be heartbroken."

"Poor Jack is a jackass."

"I don't know," Mandy said. "The more I ponder it, the more I think he's on to something. Folks will pay to see buffalo and Indians—he's right about that."

"Have you ever seen a buff up close?"

"Only from a distance. Why?"

"They are death on hooves. The males can be up to a ton of muscle, the females half that. Both have horns with a spread of up to three feet. And they can be downright vicious. Rile one, and it will gore you and trample you to a pulp."

"Only if you let it. If they're roped and hog-tied, they're harmless, just like Jack says."

"People won't pay to see a hog-tied buff."

"That's where you come in," Mandy said brightly. "Horses can be tamed and trained. Why not buffalo?"

"Are you taking Jack's side?"

Mandy came over and sat on the cot next to him. She caressed his cheek and kissed his forehead. "I'm only saying you ought to at least try to corral one buffalo. What can you lose?"

"Besides my life?"

"Do it careful. If it doesn't work, fine, you've proved Jack wrong. But if buffalo can be tamed, think of all the money we'll have."

"We?" Fargo said.

"Oh. Didn't I tell you?" Mandy looked away as if embarrassed. "While you were tending to your horse, Jack propositioned me."

"I bet."

"No, it's not what you think," Mandy said. "He mentioned as how his Extravaganza needs a lady to star in it. You know, the damsel in distress sort of thing."

"And you're his damsel."

"I'm not *his*, consarn you. But he did say he thinks I'm pretty enough that the job is mine if I want it, and he'd pay me forty dollars a month and free meals."

"Listen to you," Fargo said.

"What? I need work, don't I? I'll get to wear a fancy dress and recite some lines and be paid for it."

"So that's why."

Mandy scowled and smacked him. "Stop it. He offered me a job and that's all."

Fargo closed his eyes and started to roll over but she held on to his shoulder. "I need to get some sleep."

"No, you don't," Mandy said. "This is too important. If you won't do it for the friend who saved your life—"

"Did Jack bring that up?"

"No. He's too much of a gentleman to rub your nose in the debt you owe him."

"Gentleman, hell." Fargo was willing to bet every dollar in his poke that Jack had put her up to this.

"As I was trying to say, if you won't do it for your friend, do it for me."

"Damn it, Mandy."

"A couple weeks of your time. That's all we ask. By then we'll either have a tame buff or we won't and be no worse off than we are now."

Fargo swore some more.

"Just two more weeks," Mandy stressed, and taking his hand, she placed it on her right breast. "And you get to have me every night or whenever else you want." She ran his hand down over her stomach to the junction of her thighs and pressed his fingers between them. "What do you say? Yes or no?"

Fargo groaned.

15

The plains swarmed with buffalo, or so the Eastern newspapers would have had everyone believe. While it was true that some herds were estimated to be a million or more, finding one wasn't as easy as a greenhorn might have expected.

For starters, buffalo were nearly always on the move.

They stopped to graze and slake their thirst and to rest but for much of each day they roved. At certain times of the year they took part in migrations that covered hundreds if not thousands of miles.

Then there was the fact that sometimes the sight or scent of humans provoked a stampede. Once they started running, a herd might go for hours.

Fargo had been searching for fresh buffalo sign for three days when he came on half a dozen wallows. Several showed signs of recent use.

Fargo wasn't alone. Texas Jack was with him. Mandy had insisted on coming and while Fargo balked, Texas Jack said by all means. In addition, eight of Jack's hired hands and two of the Pawnees were along.

Now, as Fargo wound among the wallows, Texas Jack gigged his sorrel up to the Ovaro.

"I can't believe it's taking this long. If we weren't looking for them they'd be all over the place."

"This time of year," Fargo said, "most have migrated south."

"All we need are ten or so."

"How about just one to start?" Fargo said, and pointed.

A quarter of a mile away stood a solitary buffalo.

"There is a God," Texas Jack said. Shifting in the saddle, he barked commands. "Calhoun, you and the others break out the ropes. Running Bear, I'm counting on you and High Eagle to drive that brute back toward us if it breaks for the hills."

"We're nowhere near the foothills," Fargo said.

"Figure of speech," Texas Jack said. Slipping a hand under his shirt, he produced his silver flask, opened it, and chugged. "Care for some coffin varnish?"

"Not when we're about to tangle with a buff." Fargo wanted his wits about him. "You should stay sober yourself."

"I'm nearly always sober."

"And I'm a nun. The only time you're not three sheets to the wind is when you're asleep."

"I resent that," Texas Jack said, not sounding offended in the least. "But I'll overlook the slur so we can catch us a buff."

The men knew what to do. First the Pawnees circled wide until they were on the other side of their quarry.

When they were in position, the hired helpers spread out, each with a rope in his hands.

"I've drilled them good," Texas Jack flattered himself.

"Stay with Jack," Fargo said to Mandy, and caught up to the ropers. Despite himself, he wanted to see how Jack's great plan played out.

"Nice and slow, boys," Calhoun said. Unlike Jack, he was a real Texan and wore a low-crowned hat and chaps. He was a wizard with a rope. Fargo had seen him toss a loop ten times out of ten tries over the contraption Jack rigged, while riding at a gallop.

The ropers continued to spread out as they advanced so that when they were within a few hundred feet of the buffalo, they had formed a circle with the bull at the center.

Fargo stayed close to Calhoun. He had a hunch the Texan would be the first to try his luck.

The buffalo just stood there. Once it raised its massive head and regarded them with no more interest than if they were flies. Then it lowered its head again.

"Why isn't it movin'?" Calhoun wondered. "Buffs usually run when people get this close."

Fargo hadn't paid a lot of attention to the bull but now he did. It was young, not quite in its prime, but still formidable.

Its sides were moving in and out far more than normal and he could hear its labored breathing from fifty feet away.

"What do you make of it?" Calhoun asked.

Fargo was about to say he had no idea when he noticed pinkish coils in the grass underneath the buffalo. "I need to get closer."

"Watch yourself," Calhoun warned.

Fargo held the Henry across his saddle, his thumb on the hammer. He had a feeling he should know what the coils were but the truth didn't dawn until he saw splashes of red on the buffalo's legs and hindquarters and more red on the grass. Drawing rein, he twisted around. "It's hurt. There's blood everywhere and its guts are hanging out."

"What the hell?" Calhoun started toward him. "Injuns, do you reckon?"

"Wolves, most likely," was Fargo's guess. Wolf packs constantly harassed herds, culling the weak and the young.

Suddenly Calhoun stiffened and pointed. "Look out!" he cried.

Fargo heard the drum of hooves even as he turned.

The wounded bull was charging him.

16

Head lowered, horns gleaming in the sunlight, the bull swept at Fargo like a dreadnought of death. From under it trailed its intestines, whipping in the grass like a snake.

Fargo hauled on the reins and jabbed his spurs. The Ovaro responded by breaking into a gallop.

Fargo had the Henry in his other hand, a round already in the chamber, but he didn't shoot. A buff's skull was virtual armor that only the largest-caliber rifles could penetrate. And, too, it was next to impossible to hit the heart or the lungs when the buff was head-on. So he fled, the bull wheezing and pounding after him.

Texas Jack fired but the bull didn't go down.

Mandy screamed.

Fargo glanced back. The bull's horns were inches from the Ovaro. And then something incredible happened. If he hadn't seen it with his own eyes, he wouldn't have believed it.

The buffalo tripped over its own intestines. A rear leg came down on the rope of guts. The intestine split open but didn't break and somehow wrapped around the leg. The bull gave another bound and its leg was pulled out from under it and down it crashed, bellowing as it fell.

Instantly, Fargo slowed and reined around. He brought the Henry to his shoulder. He had a shot now, and he took it, firing not once but three times into the buffalo's side.

Blood gushed from the bull's nose. It tried to rise but its leg was entangled. Kicking, thrashing, it made it halfway up, then grunted, keeled onto its side, and was still.

"Damn," Fargo said.

The others converged.

Texas Jack laughed and slapped his saddle horn. "Did

you see that? Tripped over its own guts! That was the funniest thing I've seen in a coon's age."

"It wasn't so funny to me," Mandy said.

Nor to Fargo. He'd been lucky. "You and your goddamned harebrained notions, Jack."

"What did I do?" Texas Jack said. "It wasn't my fault that bull was hurt. The next one will be healthy and things will go better."

"You hope."

Texas Jack sighed. "You sure are a sour son of a gun these days."

They resumed the hunt. Jack sent the Pawnees out to sweep wide.

Mandy rode with Fargo. She was upset, and vented. "I'm beginning to see why you were against this. You were almost killed."

"Noticed that, did you?"

"Now, now. I'm mature enough to admit when I'm wrong and I might have been wrong about this."

"Might?"

"We can't give up. Not with a job for me at stake."

"You hope," Fargo said.

"Yes, I truly do. Having a little money is better than being poor. Having a lot would be better. And I wouldn't mind being famous."

"When did that happen?"

"Oh, you're so funny. Jack says when we put on the Extravaganza, folks will come from all over. The newspapers will write about us. About me. He says I'll get to wear pretty dresses, the kind that rich ladies wear. He says men will fawn over me and bring me flowers."

"Jack says a lot."

"Don't use that tone. He's your friend. He has your best interests at heart."

"You could have fooled me."

"He offered you a share of the profits, didn't he? If his show is a success you'll never want for money the rest of your days."

"If," Fargo said.

Mandy glanced at him sharply. "Jack is right. You are a bundle of sour grapes." She reined away and over toward Texas Jack.

Fargo was glad to be left alone but he wasn't for long.

A second shadow joined the Ovaro's.

"Mind if I ask you a question, mister?" Calhoun said.

"So long as it's not about dresses and fame."

"Eh?" The Texan shook his head. "It's about this whole shindig. Do you think it's as loco as I do?"

"I do," Fargo admitted. "Yet here we are."

Calhoun frowned. "It's that pard of yours. He got me half drunk and talked me into it. I kept tellin' him I wasn't interested but he wouldn't take no for an answer."

"That's Jack."

"I've been with him pretty near three weeks now and I ain't ever once seen him sober."

"That's Jack," Fargo said again.

"I gave up a good job on a ranch for this," Calhoun said. "And now I'm havin' second thoughts."

"I'm having third and fourth."

"What? Oh." Calhoun grinned. "We are a pitiful pair. Although I reckon you have a better excuse than me, what with that gal and all. I hear she's got her heart set on bein' Jack's star, as he calls her."

"Does he, now?"

"I heard them talkin' the other night. Jack was feedin' it to her with a shovel."

"That's Jack."

Calhoun cocked his head. "If you feel that way about him, what are you doin' here?"

"He saved my life once."

"Oh, hell."

"My sentiments exactly." Fargo motioned at the Texan's rope. "You ever used that on a buffalo before?"

"Who in God's name goes around ropin' buffs?"

"Do you think you can?"

"I can rope anything," Calhoun declared. "The problem will be once I get the rope around it. With a cow I know what to expect. With a buff—" He shrugged.

"Let's make a pact," Fargo said.

"A pact?"

"If this brainstorm of Jack's gets either of us killed, the other one shoots him."

Calhoun laughed. "That's a good joke, mister."

"Who's joking?" Fargo said.

17

"Oh my," Mandy said.

The herd stretched to the far horizon, thousands upon thousands. From a distance those farthest away were black specks of pepper sprinkled on a green tablecloth. Most were grazing or resting. Some were taking dust baths. Calves frolicked and nuzzled their mother's teats.

"All we have to do is get close enough," Texas Jack said, "and we'll have all we need."

"They won't stand there and let us rope them," Calhoun said.

"I have an idea about that," Texas Jack declared.

"Here we go again," Fargo said.

They were lying on a hill half a mile north of the herd. Their mounts were at the bottom of the hill, with one man watching them.

"Let's hear your idea," Mandy said.

Texas Jack slid back a few feet and sat up. Taking his flask out, he glued his mouth to it and his throat bobbed. "I needed to wash the dust down first."

"The day you need an excuse to drink," Fargo said, "is the day those buffs sprout wings and fly."

"Your idea," Mandy prompted.

Texas Jack regarded Calhoun and his other men. "Our friend from Texas has a point. We go riding down there, those critters will scatter six ways to Sunday. I propose we do it smart, like the Injuns do." He turned toward the two Pawnees. "Tell them, Running Bear."

"Tell what?" Running Bear asked.

"How Injuns go after buffalo."

"We ride. We shoot arrow. Buffalo die."

"No, not that. The other way," Texas Jack said.

Running Bear looked at High Eagle, the other Pawnee. High Eagle was young and considerably handsome. They talked in their tongue and Running Bear looked at Texas Jack. "When run buffalo over cliff?"

"No, not that, damn it. What good would buffalo be to me dead. I meant the *other* other way."

"Your head in whirl," Running Bear said.

Fargo laughed. That was the Indian way of saying someone was crazy.

Texas Jack wasn't amused. "Very well. I'll tell them myself." He turned to his other men. "Sometimes Injuns don't use horses. Sometimes they disguise themselves and sneak up on the buffalo without the buffalo catching on."

"Disguise how?" Calhoun asked skeptically.

"The pretend they are bushes."

The men stared.

"I'm serious," Texas Jack said. "I saw some Cheyenne do it once. They got hold of tumbleweeds and held the weeds in front of them and snuck right up on a bull they aimed to have for supper."

Calhoun put on a little show of rising partway and looking to the right and the left and behind them. "You see any tumbleweeds hereabouts?"

"It doesn't have to be a tumbleweed," Texas Jack said. "It can be any bush, or a tree, for that matter."

"We're in the middle of the prairie, for God's sake. There hasn't been a tree in miles."

Fargo smothered another laugh.

"All right, then," Texas Jack said. "We'll make do with what's at hand. You and the others can disguise yourselves as grass."

The men did as the Pawnees had done and looked at one another and then stared at Texas Jack.

"It's brilliant, I tell you," Jack said. "You pluck a lot of grass and stick it all over you and sneak up on the buffs."

"I want to go home," one of the men said.

"How do we make the grass stick?" Calhoun asked.

"It can't be that hard." Texas Jack plucked a thick handful of stems and proceeded to stick them up his sleeves and under the neck of his shirt and a few under his hat. "See?"

"You look plumb silly."

"The buffalo will be able to tell it's a person and not grass," Calhoun said.

"Use a lot," Texas Jack advised, and indicated the grass up his left sleeve. "This was just to demonstrate."

"I don't think it will work," another man said.

"You haven't tried it. And if you expect to get paid, you'll do as I ask."

"Hell." Calhoun began yanking grass out and sticking it into his pockets and partway down his sleeves and his shirt and under his wide-brimmed hat. The rest followed his example but didn't appear happy about it.

Texas Jack smiled. "That's the way. Put the grass everywhere you can and leave most of it poking out. Down your boots, too. And stick some out of your pants."

Presently they were done. Grass poked from every cranny in their clothes. Several had smeared grass on their faces and their cheeks and brows were green.

"Beautiful," was Texas Jack's appraisal. He nudged Fargo. "What do you think, pard?"

Fargo gave his honest opinion. "I think the first buffalo that sees them will die laughing."

18

"They're almost there!" Mandy exclaimed.

"I told you it would work," Texas Jack crowed, and treated himself to another swallow from his flask. "But you didn't believe me, did you?"

"I still don't," Fargo said. Although he had to admit, Calhoun and the others were trying their best. Slowly, with infinite care, they had worked to within a few hundred feet of the herd. So far the buffalo had ignored them.

"Oh, ye of little faith," Texas Jack said. "Once they bring a buff down, it's all over but the taming."

"*If* they can bring one down without horses," Fargo brought up. It would take a lot of doing. Buffalo were immensely strong.

Texas Jack glanced down the hill at the string. "I forgot about that."

"You forgot?" Mandy said.

"I'm not perfect. I make mistakes the same as anybody," Jack said. "Calhoun will think of something, though. Us Texans are clever that way."

"You're from Ohio," Fargo reminded him.

"I was born there, true, but my heart is the heart of a Texan."

"Poor Texas," Fargo said.

From the look of things, Calhoun and the rest of the ropers were closing on a particular buffalo. From that distance Fargo couldn't tell if it was a bull or a cow but either would prove a challenge.

"How will you go about taming it?" Texas Jack asked.

"I haven't thought about that yet."

"You better start." Texas Jack placed his hand on Fargo's shoulder. "I'm counting on you. Fail me, and this whole enterprise falls apart."

"Look!" Mandy squealed.

The ropers were in position. Calhoun was nearest to the buff. He began to swing his rope in slow circles that grew faster and wider.

The buffalo looked at him.

Fargo wished he was closer. Should the ropers need help, there was little he could do. Rising, he headed down the slope.

"Where are you going?" Texas Jack asked.

There wasn't time for Fargo to explain. He reached the string and took hold of the stallion's reins and swung up. Bending low, he snatched the reins to Calhoun's mount and to another.

"What are you doing?" the man standing guard asked.

"Maybe saving their hides." Fargo trotted around the hill leading the other two animals.

Calhoun and another roper had thrown loops over and under the buffalo and it was bucking and jumping and threatening to pull them off their feet and drag them. The other ropers were trying to add their ropes to the combined effort.

The rest of the buffalo, meanwhile, were becoming agitated.

Fargo saw a bull paw the ground. He saw a cow toss its head in a belligerent manner and move toward the buff that had been roped.

"Come back here!" Texas Jack bawled from the top of the hill. "You'll spook the herd!"

It wasn't the buffalo Fargo was concerned about; it was the men. He spurred to a gallop, his left arm straining to hold on to the other reins.

"Skye!" Mandy shouted.

Fargo had seen it.

The second man who had got a rope around the buffalo had been pulled off his feet, and Calhoun was straining to hold on.

The cow that had been tossing its head suddenly lowered it and charged.

Calhoun didn't see her. He was intent on the one he had roped. Another man shouted and Calhoun realized his peril. Fargo expected him to let go of the rope and run. Instead, the Texan threw himself flat.

At the last instant the cow veered aside.

But now the bull that had been pawing the ground was moving toward them.

Fargo raced full out. He still wasn't close enough to help. All he could do was rise in the stirrups and yell and holler to try to distract the bull. It worked. The bull stopped and looked at him and then did the last thing he wanted it to do—its huge head dipped and it came at him like a bat out of hell.

Fargo reined to the west. He kept on, confident the Ovaro could outrun any buff alive. Calhoun's horse was doing well but the other one was flagging and he had to tug on the reins. A glance showed that the bull wasn't gaining. "He'll never catch us," he said out loud.

Fargo spoke too soon. He faced front and beheld acres of mounds of dirt and dozens of dark spots in the earth. The dark spots were holes and the mounds were a prairie dog town.

A single misstep would bring the Ovaro crashing down.

19

Fargo reined to the right to go around. In doing so he lost ground to the bull.

The mounds and holes stretched on and on.

Anxious to get past them and leave the bull in the dust, Fargo rose in the stirrups. The end of the town was hundreds of yards away. The bull was less than half that and swiftly gaining. He wouldn't reach the open prairie before the bull reached him.

His plight called for a desperate gambit. Fargo hated to put the Ovaro at risk but in a choice between being gored by a bull or possibly breaking a leg by stepping into a prairie dog burrow, he chose the slightly lesser of the two.

Waiting until the very last moment, until the bull was almost on them, Fargo let go of the reins to the other two horses and reined into the prairie dog colony. Immediately, a hole was in front of them. He reined sharply left to avoid it. Another and another appeared. The stallion responded superbly to every pull of the reins.

Behind them came a loud crack and a startled bellow from their pursuer.

Fargo glanced back and brought the Ovaro to a stop.

The bull was down. It had stepped in a hole and its front leg was stuck fast. Now it was struggling to straighten and stand.

Fargo warily circled, watching for holes.

Grunting and bellowing, the bull righted itself. It heaved erect but its leg was still caught. Tugging and wrenching, it finally tugged free—and almost toppled when it put its weight on the hurt leg. The white of bone gleamed through ruptured hide. Its leg had snapped like a twig.

The bull took another step, or tried to. Stumbling, it raised the stricken limb and stood on the other three. It looked at Fargo and tossed its head in fury.

Fargo knew what was in store. The buff might last a week or more but eventually hunger and thirst would bring it down—if hungry wolves didn't find it first. He drew rein and raised the Henry. The camp could always use the meat. He lined the sights for a heart shot, held his breath to steady his aim, and when he was sure, stroked the trigger. He thought it might take more than one but the bull dropped like a poled ox.

As the blast faded, thunder rumbled. To the south the herd had broke into motion. Thousands of hooves were churning the sod and raising a thick cloud of dust.

One of the herd wasn't going anywhere. It was on its side with ropes around its legs and another over its head. Calhoun and the other ropers had done it; they'd caught one.

Fargo made his careful way to safe ground. He collected the two horses and headed for the Texan.

Jack and Mandy came around the hill, Jack yelling something or other.

Calhoun smiled tiredly as Fargo drew rein, his face caked with sweat and dust. "I'm obliged for the save. That bull might have done me in."

The cow they had roped was attempting to stand but they had the ropes taut and she couldn't roll upright. Her eyes wide with fear, she snorted and kicked.

Fargo climbed down. He held on to the Henry. Should the cow break loose, he'd need it.

"I've done some boneheaded stunts in my day," Calhoun said, "but this about beats all."

"You caught one," Fargo complimented him.

"And damn near got drug off and stomped." Calhoun shook his head. "The next one Jack can rope himself."

"Speak of the devil," Fargo said.

Texas Jack and Mandy were there. Jack was off the horse before it stopped moving and ran to the cow and let out a whoop. "I did it, by God! I've got me a buff!"

"You had help," Fargo said drily.

Texas Jack took out his flask, raised it to the sky in salute, and drank. Capping it, he put it back in his pocket, bent, and patted the cow's hind end. "My very own bull."

"Look again, Jack," Fargo said.

Jack bent farther. "A cow? I was so excited I didn't notice. Not that it matters. This is just the first of many. Soon we'll have our very own herd."

"You hope," Calhoun said.

Mandy gazed at the cow with trepidation. "Can it really be tamed down?"

"Anything can, missy," Texas Jack said. "I knew a gent once who had a pet grizzly."

Fargo knew the same man. "Which he kept muzzled except when it was in its cage. One day it broke out and mauled him and had to be shot."

"He should have had a stronger cage," Jack said. Squatting, he touched the cow's leg and she thrashed and almost kicked him. "Isn't she a beauty?"

"A minute ago you thought she was a he," Calhoun said.

"Let's get her back to the pen."

It proved to be as hard as Fargo figured it would.

They tied ropes to each of the cow's four legs. Fargo, Calhoun, and two others then each took one of the ropes and dallied them around their saddle horns. The cow was allowed to stand. She stood shaking herself and glaring, then exploded into motion, charging one of the riders. Instantly, Fargo and Calhoun tightened their ropes and brought her crashing down.

"Careful!" Texas Jack hollered. "Don't break her leg! We don't want her hurt."

"What about us?" a man asked.

Jack didn't answer.

The cow got up and did the same thing. Again. And again.

Fargo was beginning to wonder if she would keep at it all day.

"Wait," Texas Jack yelled. "I have a brainstorm."

"Not another one," Calhoun said.

Texas Jack went to his horse, untied his bedroll, and unfolded a blanket. He took a swallow from his flask, then advanced on the cow holding the blanket in front of him.

"What in hell do you think you're doing?" Fargo demanded.

"They do this with bulls in Mexico," Jack said. "If I can get this over her head so she can't see, she'll come along as meek as a lamb."

"Please don't," Mandy said.

"Keep those ropes tight, boys." Texas Jack grinned and advanced and flapped the blanket practically in the cow's face.

"Oh, God," Fargo said.

The cow attacked.

20

Fargo tried to keep his rope taut. So did Calhoun and the others. But the cow covered the few yards in a couple of bounds and rammed into Texas Jack Lavender with her head low.

Mandy screamed.

Fargo couldn't see much for the blanket. It fell over the cow's head and the next thing, Texas Jack somersaulted through the air. Jack landed and rolled and wound up on his stomach with his face in the dirt.

The cow stood still, the blanket over her head, her horns poking through.

"Jack!" Mandy cried, rushing over.

"Keep the ropes tight," Fargo shouted to the other ropers.

Mandy reached Texas Jack and pressed her hands to her throat and cried, "Oh, God."

Jack sat up. He looked down at himself, then at the cow with the blanket over her head, then touched his chest and his belly, and laughed. "Nothing is broken, by God. And I don't have any holes in me." He whooped and pulled out his flask. "This calls for a celebration."

"I could shoot him," Calhoun said.

The cow tossed her head to shed the blanket but her horns were stuck.

Texas Jack got to his feet. Mandy hugged him, and he let go of her and came over to the cow, and chortled. "Look at her. It worked like a charm."

The cow tilted her head as if trying to locate him by the sound of his voice.

"Watch out," Calhoun warned.

"She can't go after what she can't see," Texas Jack assured him.

The cow lowered her head and charged. Or tried to. The ropes kept her from moving.

"See?" Texas Jack said.

To everyone's considerable amazement, the cow became docile. They threw another rope over her head and neck and led her toward camp. Calhoun did the leading. Two others rode by her side and Fargo came after her in case she tried to break away.

Once she was in the pen and the gate was closed, Calhoun brought up the obvious.

"Someone has to get that blanket off."

Running Bear volunteered to do it if he was paid extra.

Texas Jack grumbled but agreed. They held the gate open while Running Bear crept up to the cow, gripped the blanket, and tugged. It was stuck fast. He tugged again, harder. One horn came free and the blanket slid partway down, uncovering an eye. She glared at the Pawnee.

"Run, you red lunkhead," a man named Lefty bawled.

Running Bear whirled and fled with the cow after him. He didn't bother with the gate. He dashed straight at the fence, leaped high, caught hold of the top rail, and was up and over. The cow didn't stop. The fence shook but held and she fell back on her haunches and moved her head back and forth, dazed, the blanket flapping from one side of her head to the other.

"We sure showed her," Texas Jack said.

Fargo spied the cook among the onlookers. Horace Schumer was the man's name, and if he wasn't the worst cook in creation, he was close to it. Schumer also supplied Texas Jack, and anyone else with the money to pay for it, with whiskey. Fargo marched over. "I want a bottle."

"Get it for you a minute," Schumer said. He was fascinated by the buffalo.

"Now."

Muttering, Schumer made for the cook tent. "It'll cost you five dollars."

"That's robbery," Fargo said. A gallon of whiskey could be had at any saloon for less than a dollar.

"You're welcome to head into town and buy from someone else," Schumer said smugly.

Fargo knew full well there wasn't a watering hole within three hundred miles. "Do you charge Texas Jack that much?" At the rate Jack sucked the bug juice down, Fargo didn't see how he could afford it.

"Jack gets his free," Schumer said, "in return for me being able to charge everyone else as much as I want."

"Figures," Fargo said.

Half an hour later over half the bottle was gone and Fargo lay on his cot watching a fly buzz around the tent post. As he raised the bottle to his lips, the flap opened and in came Mandy.

"Jack wants to see you."

"I'm busy."

"He says he'd like for you to start taming that buffalo."

"Would he, now?" Fargo swallowed and luxuriated in a feeling of peace and contentment. "Give old Jack a message for me."

"Certainly. What is it?"

"Tell him to take his head in both of his hands . . ."

"Yes?"

". . . and shove it up his ass."

Mandy put her hand on her hips. "What's the matter? You came all this way to help him and now you're refusing to lend a hand?"

"I helped catch the cow."

"He's counting on you to tame her. He says no one but you can do it."

"Jack can talk an Apache out of his moccasins. He'll say anything to get what he wants. Be careful or he'll talk his way up your dress."

"Honestly," Mandy said, blushing. "He's always been a gentleman around me."

"Just wait," Fargo said.

"How can you talk about him like that? He's your best friend."

"One of them," Fargo admitted. "He's also a drunk and a jackass."

Mandy stared at the bottle in Fargo's hand. "You're a fine one to talk."

"Go away."

"I will not. He sent me to fetch you and that's exactly what I'm going to do." Mandy tugged at his leg. "Come on. He's at the pen, waiting."

On second thought, Fargo decided to go. He'd give Jack a piece of his mind and light a shuck. Mandy could come or she could stay, her choice. He corked the bottle, slid it under the cot, and stood.

"That's better," Mandy said. She opened the flap. "Be sure to bring your saddle."

"For what?"

"Didn't you know? Capturing that buff was only part of it. Jack wants you to throw your saddle on and ride her."

21

Texas Jack was by the gate, grinning at his prize. "About time. What kept you?"

Fargo slugged him. Not with all his strength but hard enough that Jack tottered on his boot heels and clutched at the rails.

"What the hell? You damn near busted my teeth."

"I can do it again," Fargo said.

Texas Jack held his hands up, palms out. "Whoa there, hoss. I don't want to fight you. We're pards, remember?"

"What's this about me riding that damn buff?"

"Imagine it," Jack said, grinning. "I announce the Texas Jack Extravaganza—"

"I thought it was the Great Frontier Extravaganza?"

"Since it was my idea and I'm the star, it's only right the show be named after me." Texas Jack motioned. "Now imagine. I come out in front of the audience and talk about the show we're about to put on. Just when I have them excited as can be, you ride out on a buffalo. They'll go wild, I tell you. They'll never have seen anything like it."

"You ever see Indians riding buffalo?"

"Sometimes you make no sense. Injuns ride horses. No one ever rides buffalo. That's why it will be a sensation. The newspapers will write it up. People will flock to see for themselves and we'll have more money than we'll know what to do with."

"You like the idea so much," Fargo said, "*you* ride the buffalo."

"You think I won't try? You think I'm yellow?"

"No, I'd never think that," Fargo admitted. His friend had more than his share of faults but cowardice wasn't one of them. "You're just loco."

71

"Why does everyone keep saying that?" Jack rubbed his hands together. "How about if I make it worth your while? A thousand dollars from the proceeds is yours if you'll train this buff to the saddle and get her used to being ridden."

"My life is worth more to me than money. I'll try to tame her but I'll be damned if you can talk me into riding her."

"Two thousand, then?"

"How much money do you expect to make?"

They were interrupted by the youngest Pawnee who stepped forward and announced in poor English, "Me ride *taraha*."

"Tara-what?" Mandy said.

"It's Pawnee for 'buffalo,'" Fargo explained.

Texas Jack regarded the volunteer skeptically. "Why in hell do you want to do it, High Eagle, when the best rider I know won't?"

"For money," High Eagle said. "Me hear you say. Thousand dollars be mine."

Texas Jack pulled out his flask and drank and wiped his mouth with the back of his hand. "It wouldn't be quite that much."

"How much?" High Eagle asked.

"A thousand dollars is how much I'm willing to give my pard. Skye and me are like blood brothers. You savvy?"

"Oh brother," Fargo said.

"Me savvy," High Eagle said.

"You might call that my pard rate," Texas Jack went on. "Then there's the white rate and the black rate even though we don't have any blacks and then there's the red rate."

"Red rate?"

"How much I'm willing to pay. In your case it's five—" Texas Jack caught himself. "In your case it's two hundred dollars, cash or credit, my choice."

"Only two hundred?" High Eagle didn't hide his disappointment.

"There's nothing 'only' about it. Two hundred is a lot. You can buy a new rifle and pistol or a horse or blankets or trinkets for the gals you're courting."

Fargo couldn't resist. "Does he get two hundred every show he rides in?"

Texas Jack shot him an annoyed glance. "No. It's two hundred for the season."

"What be season?" High Eagle said.

"For however long the show lasts," Texas Jack clarified. "If it catches on like I suspect, that could be several moons or more."

High Eagle digested this and said, "Me do for three hundred for season."

"I wouldn't do it for less than four hundred," Fargo said, smiling at Jack.

"What him say," High Eagle said. "It now four hundred."

Texas Jack's jaw muscles twitched. "Skye, don't you have something to do?" He smiled and went up to High Eagle and put his arm around the young warrior's shoulders. "Let's you and me go hash this out over a bottle. What do you say?"

"Me say four hundred."

"I would love to pay you that much. I truly would," Texas Jack said as he led the Pawnee off. "But I have expenses to consider. Do you know what they are? And then there's my overhead and my underhead and my in-betweens."

"What?" High Eagle said.

"I'll explain everything . . ."

Their voices trailed off.

Fargo swore and stepped to the fence and leaned on the top rail. The cow was half an acre away, peacefully grazing, the blanket still stuck on one horn. "This can't get any more stupid."

"Well, I think it's exciting," Mandy said. "Capturing that thing, and now someone is going to ride it. And tomorrow Calhoun is going back out to rope some more." She clasped her hands. "I've never been so thrilled about anything."

"I need my bottle," Fargo said.

22

Everyone came to watch. They lined the rails on both sides of the gate. The two Pawnees stood slightly apart. Running Bear looked worried.

Calhoun and a man called Travers rode up with coiled ropes in their hands. Texas Jack barked orders and another man opened the gate and the pair entered the enclosure.

Mandy squealed and clapped. "There they go. And that buff is just standing there."

Fargo hadn't taken his eyes off the cow. She raised her head but showed no alarm. She went on chewing, her one eye on the riders, the blanket down around her front hooves.

"You ever noticed how noble buffalo are?" Mandy asked.

"If you say so."

"I'm serious. Buffalo are majestic. A painter should do them on canvas. Or their likeness should be stamped on a coin."

"Why not stamp Indians while we're at it?" Fargo said.

Calhoun and Travers separated to come at the cow from opposite sides. She continued to chew as if she didn't have a care in the world until they started to uncoil their ropes. Then she wheeled and headed farther into the pen, prancing along with her head high.

"Did you see that?" Mandy said.

"I'm right here."

"She's toying with them, just like a lady toys with a suitor. Who says buffalo are dumb brutes? She has as much personality as my cat used to."

"Did that cow kick you in the head when I wasn't looking?" Fargo said.

"What's that supposed to mean?" Mandy stiffened. "Oh, look. They're about to try."

The cow had bent her muzzle to the grass. Calhoun chose that moment to rein in and throw his loop. It settled over half of her head but snagged on the horn and the blanket, and at the touch of it, the cow bounded straight up and came down with all four legs rigid. Turning, she snorted and lowered her head and barreled at Calhoun's mount. He deftly reined away. The cow went another thirty feet and dug in her hooves. Wheeling, she was about to go at him again when Travers threw his loop. It settled over both her horns and the blanket. Like Calhoun, Travers had experience with cattle, and he was quick to make the rope taut. The cow didn't like that. She flew toward his horse like a battering ram. Travers tried to rein aside as Calhoun had done but his horse wasn't as quick.

"Look out!" Mandy bawled.

The horns caught Travers's claybank low in the belly. The cow ripped upward and the claybank's intestines spilled out, along with a gush of fluids.

Fargo's legs carried him over the fence before he realized what he was doing. "Jump clear!"

Travers kicked free of both stirrups, pushed against his saddle, and threw himself to the ground just as the claybank tilted and toppled. Everyone saw him try to roll away. He thrust his hands up as the claybank crashed down—on top of him.

Calhoun vaulted from his saddle. He grabbed at a forearm sticking from under the claybank but couldn't pull Travers out. He looked around for help and saw Fargo and beckoned for him to hurry.

The cow saw Fargo, too.

Fargo's only thought had been to help. Now here he was, forty feet from the gate, and the cow thundered toward him. He couldn't reach the fence before she reached him. He swooped his hand to his Colt.

The cow was gaining speed. The blanket flapped wildly, the rope trailing after her.

"Run!" Mandy screeched.

Fargo raised the Colt. A head shot was pointless. Her

skull was too thick. He decided to go for a leg to try to bring her down.

Whether it was the blanket or the rope was hard to say but one or the other or both became entangled in the cow's legs. They buckled and she pitched into a forward roll. Her head and her tail changed places. Then she was on her side with the rope around her front legs and her rear legs kicking in impotent anger.

Fargo went around.

Calhoun was straining to pull Travers out. His face was a beet and the veins in his neck and temples stood out. "Help me," he croaked.

Planting himself, Fargo gripped the arm. "Together, on three," he said, and counted.

It was no use. The arm wouldn't budge. The claybank was too heavy.

"He never let out a peep," Calhoun said.

Fargo let go and straightened. The only thing to do was tie ropes to the claybank and drag it off the body.

"God Almighty," Calhoun said, and took a step back.

Travers's fingers were moving.

Fargo took charge. He bellowed for men to bring horses and ropes and when half a dozen came through the gate he had two of them make sure the buffalo was thoroughly hogtied and had the rest secure their ropes to the claybank. As he was about to give the command for them to pull, he hesitated.

"I know what you're thinkin'," Calhoun said. "Draggin' it off could crush him."

The fingers were twitching like crazy.

Fargo slashed the air and said, "Now!" The riders resorted to their spurs and their animals strained against the ropes. For a few seconds the claybank didn't move. Then, with a lurch, the claybank slid on its own gore and guts and went on sliding, its innards greasing the grass.

"I'll be damned," Calhoun said.

Travers was curled into a ball in a depression barely big enough for a washbasin. Gasping for breath, he rolled onto his back and clawed at the sky. "Thank God," he breathed.

Fargo and Calhoun helped him to his feet.

"Anything busted?" the Texan asked.

"No, but I might just quit," Travers said, dabbing at smears of gore. "That walkin' whiskey well can't pay me enough to put up with this. Tamin' a buff. Who ever heard of such a thing?"

Someone coughed, and they turned to find Schumer grinning and rocking on his heels. "Gentlemen."

"What the hell do you want?" Fargo said.

"It's not time for supper yet," Calhoun said.

"It's not food I want to talk about." Schumer pointed at the buffalo. "It's her."

"You want to carve her up for a meal?"

"No. It's about this taming and riding business." Schumer showed his yellow teeth. "I know how you can do it."

23

Schumer, it turned out, had been raised on a dairy farm.

His pa had had forty cows and a bull. "That bull was the meanest critter in all creation," he informed them. "It was so contrary, my pa came damn near blowing its brains out. But bulls cost a lot of money, so he had to figure another way to keep it in line."

"What did he do?" Fargo prompted.

The other buffalo wranglers had gathered around to hear the tale.

Schumer enjoyed having an audience. He puffed out his chest and hooked his thumbs in his pants. "My pa was smart as a whip. He got our chickens to lay the biggest eggs in the county and our cows to give twice as much milk as any others."

"The bull," Fargo said to keep him on track. "Or are you blowing smoke?"

"Gospel truth," Schumer said, and crossed himself. "My pa's trick worked on our bull and it will by God work on a buff."

"This year," Fargo said.

Schumer looked around to be sure everyone was listening. "All you have to do is get her drunk."

"Step aside," Calhoun said to Fargo. "I'm fixin' to punch him in the mouth."

"No, honest," Schumer said. "Let me whip up a batch and you'll see for yourselves."

"A batch of what?"

Schumer mixed water and grass and corn mash in the largest cooking pot he had until it was the consistency of oatmeal. Green oatmeal. Schumer then added whiskey, stirring slowly. He used an entire bottle—every last drop.

"What a waste of good coffin varnish," Calhoun said.

"One bottle won't hardly do it," Schumer said. "Not with an animal that size."

Fargo wasn't the only one who looked on longingly as a second bottle was upended.

At Schumer's request, two men carried the pot into the enclosure.

"Now someone has to free the buff."

Fargo took it on himself. He went in on foot. He had gone a short way when Calhoun rode up.

"In case you have to get out of here in a hurry," the Texan said.

Fargo cautiously approached. The cow had been quiet for a while and didn't raise her head when he knelt. But she watched him with the intensity of a hawk watching prey.

"She'll be after you the moment that rope is off," Calhoun predicted.

The blanket was still impaled on a horn. Fargo wanted to remove it but she was lying on one end. He slowly unraveled the rope around her legs, talking to her as he would to the Ovaro. "There, there, girl. I'm on your side. We can be friends if you quit trying to kill us." And other things just so she would become accustomed to his voice.

"Careful," Calhoun said.

Fargo was almost done. A couple of loops and her legs would be free. He unwound the second to last and she raised her head, her eyes on him. "How I let myself get talked into this I will never know," Fargo said. He removed the last loop. The cow didn't move. Warily rising, he backed toward Calhoun's horse. "We're friends now. Pretend you're a real cow and don't come after me."

The buff looked at her legs. She moved them as if to be sure she could.

Whirling, Fargo grabbed hold of Calhoun's arm. The Texan swung him up behind him and Calhoun's horse took off as if it had been jabbed with a lance.

In an explosion of motion, the cow was up and after them.

Stubbs and a friend of his by the name of Evans were holding the gate open. They and everyone else bawled for Fargo and Calhoun to hurry.

"What the hell do they think we're doin'?" Calhoun growled, lashing his reins.

Fargo looked back. The buff was coming on fast. He wanted to shoot her; she was more trouble than she was worth. They reached the gate and flew out and Evans and Stubbs swung it shut barely in time. For a harrowing second or two it appeared the cow was going to crash into it but she came to a stop and glared at it and at them.

"You're not going anywhere, Myrtle," Stubbs said, and cackled.

"Why'd you call her that?" a man asked.

"That was my wife's name. She left me for a drummer."

"Myrtle it is," Calhoun said. "We should have something to call her if she's going to be around awhile."

"Dang," a third man said. "I was hoping to name her after my ma. She was the sweetest gal you ever met."

Everyone looked at him.

"Well, she was."

Fargo slid down and stepped to the gate. "She should have a last name too."

"How come?" Evans asked.

Fargo shrugged. "We do. How about if we call her Myrtle Lavender."

The men chuckled and laughed.

"Mrs. Myrtle Lavender," one said. "We should find us a parson and do it right."

"They can go on a honeymoon," suggested another, which caused more mirth.

Myrtle sniffed, and sniffed again. She tilted her head and moved to the pot. Lowering her muzzle, she dipped her tongue into the concoction. Evidently she liked it because she began to drink in earnest.

"It's workin'!" someone whooped.

"That remains to be seen," Fargo said.

24

Myrtle drank and drank, the lap of her tongue loud and continuous. So were her grunts. As the level fell she forced her head deeper and deeper into the pot until she had pressed it in as far as it could go.

"I told you she would like it," Schumer boasted.

The lapping stopped. Myrtle had drunk the pot empty.

She grunted and raised her head, and the pot rose, too. It covered the lower half of her face almost to her eyes. She shook her head but the pot stayed on.

"It's stuck!" Stubbs exclaimed.

Myrtle walked in a circle, shaking and tossing. The pot didn't come off. She rubbed it on the ground. It stayed on her head.

"This buff tamin' is a wonderment," Travers said.

"I'd believe anything with this outfit," Calhoun said.

So would Fargo. The cow was growing more agitated. She bent her front legs as if to lie down and banged the pot against the ground, wedging it tighter.

"My pa's bull never did anything like this," Schumer said. "Buffalo sure are dumb."

"Look at her now," Stubbs said.

Myrtle was swaying. She took a few staggering steps, righted herself, and swayed some more.

"It's my brew," Schumer said. "It's taking effect."

A loud belch came from the pot.

"That gal ain't got no manners," a man joked.

Myrtle walked in a circle, belched again, and oozed onto her side.

"Is she goin' to sleep?"

"Looks like it."

Fargo opened the gate. The cow's eyes were open but glazed. He wondered if maybe they had poisoned her, but no, she was breathing normally. Taking the bull by the horns, so to speak, he gripped the edge of the pot and pulled. "Damn."

"Let me help." Calhoun had followed him in.

Together, they tugged and pried. The pot resisted their efforts.

"If anyone ever told me I'd be squattin' here one day tryin' to get a cookin' pot off a drunk buff, I'd have said they were addlepated," Calhoun said. "What do we do?"

Fargo drummed his fingers on the pot. Grease, or butter, would loosen it, only they couldn't get their fingers between the pot and Myrtle's head. "Fetch a rope."

Myrtle belched.

Fargo saw that the blanket, while still impaled, wasn't pinned under her, like before. A sharp wrench and it was off. He threw it aside.

Calhoun returned on the run. "I don't see what good this will do," he said, handing the rope over.

"We have to get her to lift her head," Fargo said as he fashioned a loop and adjusted it so it was wide enough. "Raise the pot as high as you can."

Calhoun had to strain to get it even half an inch off the ground. "Damn, she's heavy."

Fargo slipped the loop under and nodded at the Texan for him to let go. Standing, he moved around the cow's head, hunkered, and gripped both horns. They were smooth as glass and cool to the touch but as rigid as iron.

"You're not?" Calhoun said.

"Be ready to slide the rope as high as it will go."

Bunching his shoulders, Fargo exerted every muscle. The best he could do was lift her head a fraction.

"What if we poke her?" Calhoun suggested, and patted the hilt of his knife.

Fargo kicked her on her hump. Myrtle grunted and moved her head but didn't raise it. He kicked her harder. She bellowed into the pot and her eye swiveled in its socket and she twisted her neck to try to see what had struck her.

"Now," Fargo said.

Calhoun slipped the rope over the pot and quickly slid it

higher so that it was just below the rim. He pulled to tighten it and grinned and smacked the pot. "We did it. Now all we have to do is pull it off."

"Look out," Fargo said, backpedaling

Myrtle was heaving up off the grass.

Calhoun scrambled out of her reach and they both turned to run.

For all her bulk, Myrtle was fast. She was upright and pawing the ground before they went six feet.

"Stand still," Fargo urged, taking his own advice, "and maybe she won't charge."

Myrtle swung her head, and the pot, from one of them to the other.

"Easy does it," Fargo said soothingly. "We're only trying to help."

"You're forgettin' she's female," Calhoun said. "Bein' contrary is her nature."

As if to prove him right, Myrtle spread her legs in a fighting stance.

25

Fargo figured they were in for it. They couldn't reach the gate before Myrtle reached them. He stopped and tensed to leap aside. Calhoun ran on. Drawn by his movement, Myrtle made for the Texan. Fargo opened his mouth to shout a warning but it proved unnecessary. The cow took another bound and collapsed, her whole body quivering.

Calhoun stopped, and laughed. "She's drunk, by God. She can't stay up."

Fargo got hold of the rope the Texan had dropped and unraveled it as far as the gate. He had six men seize hold, and at his command, they all pulled. There was a *plop* and the cooking pot came off Myrtle's head and fell with a bang.

"We're geniuses," Schumer said.

"We?" Fargo said.

"Now comes the important part," Schumer said. "You have to go sit with her and talk to her and pet her."

"Not while I'm sober," Fargo said.

"That's how my pa tamed our bull. It has to grow used to you."

Behind them an angry voice demanded, "What have you dimwits done to my buffalo?"

Texas Jack Lavender had returned, and High Eagle was at his side.

"You killed her, didn't you?" Jack said. "I turned my back for a few minutes and you went and put her down."

"Do you see any blood?" Fargo said. "Did you hear a shot? She'd not dead. She's drunk."

"She's what?"

Schumer puffed out his chest. "It was my idea, boss. You

get Myrtle drunk, she'll do just about anything. Look at her out there, sleeping as peaceful as a baby."

"Who the hell is Myrtle?"

"She is," Schumer said, indicating the cow. "We named her. So when you put on your Extravaganza, you can introduce her as Myrtle, the Friendly Buffalo."

"And have everyone think she's tame? Have you taken leave of your senses?"

Schumer was confused. "But I thought you wanted her tame so someone can ride her?"

"I do, you idiot. But we don't want the paying public to know that. They have to think she's wild and can turn on us at any moment. Don't you see? It adds excitement, and that's why they come." Texas Jack scratched his chin. "No, Myrtle the Friendly Buffalo won't do." He snapped his fingers and smiled. "I have it. We'll still call her Myrtle. That's as good a name as any. But we'll bill her as Myrtle, the Terror of the Prairie."

"Gosh," Schumer said. "You sure have a way with words."

"You haven't heard anything yet," Texas Jack said. "When we do our shows, we'll paint the tips of her horns red to make people think it's blood."

"God Almighty. You're a genius, too."

Fargo could take only so much. He shouldered through to Mandy and grasped her hand. "Come with me." Without waiting for her to answer, he made for their tent.

"Why do you sound so mad?"

"There are people I'd like to shoot and can't."

"You should be happy at how well things are going," Mandy said. "Now that we've learned to tame Myrtle, we can tame a whole herd."

"Drunk isn't tame," Fargo said.

"It's a start. She can't gore anyone if she's seeing double."

They had left the tent flap open. Fargo ushered her in and entered and tied the flap behind them.

"What on earth are you doing? I'm not ready to go to bed yet. It's too early."

Fargo turned and cupped her breasts. "Three guesses."

"Oh my," Mandy said. "In broad daylight with everyone about?" Mandy's eyes sparkled with mischievous delight.

"If you don't want to, say so."

Mandy giggled and cupped his chin. "The day I don't want to is the day I'm dead."

A girl after Fargo's own heart. He molded his mouth to hers and she inserted her tongue. Under his hands her breasts swelled and her nipples hardened. He pressed against her and she ground her nether mount against his manhood.

Over at the pen, Texas Jack was bellowing something or other. Fargo didn't give a damn. The whole affair was a circus he'd as soon forget about for a while. He kissed Mandy's right ear and traced the tip of his tongue from her lobe to her throat.

"Mmmmmm, I like that," Mandy whispered.

Holding her so she wouldn't fall, Fargo moved her to the cot and eased her onto her back.

Mandy grinned and opened her arms and spread her legs. "You really want to, don't you?"

Hiking at her dress, Fargo ran his hand up her long leg to her satiny thigh. Her skin was warm to his touch. Rubbing and massaging, he slowly worked higher. His knuckles brushed her slit and she arched her back like a she-cat in heat and puckered her rosy lips in a delectable oval.

"Take me, handsome. I am all yours."

Fargo wished she would stop jabbering. Cupping her bottom, he rubbed up and down. Her arousal grew. She fastened her lips to his and sucked on his tongue. Her fingers probed from his shoulders to his waist, and lower. She cupped him, and a lump formed in his throat.

A flick of Fargo's finger provoked a shiver. She dug her nails into his arms as her mouth left wet marks across his neck to his jaw.

"I want you," Mandy whispered.

Fargo was feeling the need, himself. He started on her buttons, a row that would take forever to undo. He had half a mind to rip the dress off but contained himself. She'd be mad, and it would spoil her mood.

Mandy undid his pants and his member bulged. "Oh my," she said, and touched him.

Fargo heard more bellowing. Something had Texas Jack bothered. He refused to listen. He lathered Mandy's neck and moved lower until he was at a breast. Taking the nipple into his mouth, he swirled it.

Mandy was eager with need. She stroked him. She kissed his chest and his flat belly. She bent and delicately nipped.

Fargo slowly inserted the tip of his pole. Her velvet walls sheathed him. When he was all the way in, he lay still. She didn't. She rocked gently and raked her fingernails from his shoulders to his buttocks. She wasn't gentle. It was a delicious hurt.

"Ah," Mandy said softly, and closed her eyes and shook. "I'm there."

Fargo wasn't. He dipped his wick, gradually moving faster. He was at it a long while.

Mandy matched his rhythm. By her expressions she appeared to enjoy it even more than he did. The next time she shook, it was an earthquake.

Fargo gripped the cot's frame. He was almost to the pinnacle. A few more thrusts, and a keg of powder detonated between his legs. He rammed and slammed. She was soft and yielding and buoyant, like a lily. He thought the cot would break but it held together.

Afterward, Fargo rested on his side. Her chin was at his neck and he felt the flutter of her breath. She fell asleep. He didn't intend to but he dozed, too.

A feeling woke him, a sense that eyes were on them, that they were being watched. He opened his eyes and raised his head from the cot. No one could look in with the flap tied and he recollected tying it.

Only now it wasn't.

Fargo rose on an elbow. It was possible the tie had come undone. In his hunger to have her, he might not have tied it tight enough. Easing off so as not to wake her, he put his clothes as they should be.

A breeze moved the flap. Fargo peered out but no one was near. A commotion was taking place down by the buffalo enclosure, but what else was new? He closed the flap and retied it and sat on the cot.

Mandy was a vision. In sleep her face was beautiful, her lips ripe cherries.

A stealthy sound brought Fargo around with his hand on

his Colt. There was no mistaking it for anything else; it had been a footfall. Someone was out there. He opened the flap and went out and stood with his back to it, wondering what in hell was going on. He sidled toward a corner just as someone came rushing around it. They nearly collided.

"What the hell?" Evans blurted.

"I could say the same," Fargo said.

"Calhoun sent me," Evans said, breathless from running. "You have to come quick."

"Why?"

"Texas Jack is hurt."

26

There was blood but not much. Texas Jack was on his back, surrounded by his men. He was cursing them and their mothers and demanding they leave him be.

They parted for Fargo. He saw the nick on Jack's left cheek and the dirt on Jack's buckskins and a bruise on Jack's forehead and put two and two together. "You tried to ride the buff yourself, didn't you?"

Calhoun was on his knees, muttering to himself. "The damned fool. He says he's goin' to try again. I reckoned you might talk sense into him."

"Who is in charge here?" Texas Jack demanded, propping his elbows under him.

"I thought High Eagle volunteered," Fargo said. He looked around for the young Pawnee and spied Myrtle. She was looking mad as hell, and had a saddle on her back. She also had a length of rope around her neck for use as a bridle. "Now I've seen everything," he said.

"I said I was going to, didn't I?" Texas Jack retorted. "We got it on her while she was passed out from the booze."

"She threw him," Calhoun said. "He was damned lucky she didn't gore him, too."

At that moment Schumer and two other men hurried up bearing the large pot, which once again brimmed with green mash. "Here's the new batch, boss," Schumer said. "Where do you want us to put it?"

Texas Jack stiffly rose and swatted at the dirt and grass on his buckskins. He raised an arm and pointed off across the prairie. "Why don't you take it off about a mile and set it down?"

"Really?"

"No, not really, you stupid son of a bitch. Where do you think I want it? In the pen so she can drink it."

"Oh."

Several men jumped to open the gate. Nervous as mice caught in the open near a cat, Schumer and two others hastily deposited the pot inside, never once taking their eyes off Myrtle. She glowered and snorted but didn't charge. When the gate swung shut, she sniffed and came to the pot and lowered her muzzle.

"I used three bottles this time," Schumer said. "She'll be so tipsy she won't know up from down."

"I wish I was her," Lefty remarked. "I wouldn't mind being sloshed."

Neither would Fargo. A good rip-roaring falling-down drunk would do wonders for his mood.

Myrtle drank the pot dry, the same as last time. Only she didn't get her head stuck. She walked off a short way and commenced to sway while gazing at the sky and at the ground and off into the distance.

"Even her brain is drunk," Evans said.

"She's ready to be ridden," Texas Jack said, and stepped to the gate to open it.

High Eagle put a hand on his arm. "You say me can ride. For money."

"And you will," Texas Jack said. "But I'm the boss and I should try first."

"If you break neck, who pay me?" High Eagle said.

"I break my neck, no one gets paid."

"Better me try."

Some of the men spoke up. They agreed with the Pawnee.

As Schumer put it, "This whole business is your doing, boss. Without you it'll fall apart. Let him do the riding. You're too important."

"I am, aren't I?" Texas Jack turned to Fargo. "What do you think?"

"I think you should ride her. A fall on the head might knock some sense into you."

"Do you, now? You'll change your tune once the money starts rolling in." Texas Jack nodded at High Eagle. "Very well. I have to put the welfare of the men first. You can ride her. Just be careful."

"Me not get hurt," High Eagle said.

"It's not you I'm worried about," Texas Jack said. "I don't want anything to happen to her."

They opened the gate and High Eagle went in. His shoulders were back and he moved stiffly, as if sure he was walking to his doom.

Myrtle didn't notice.

High Eagle circled to come up behind her. When he reached her, he spoke softly and touched her. She didn't react. He rubbed her side and her back and then her neck.

Myrtle turned her head and looked at him.

Everyone froze. This was the moment. Either she would try to kill him or she was so booze blind, she'd let him do whatever he wanted.

Myrtle grunted.

High Eagle slowly bent and picked up the rope. He slowly straightened and turned to the saddle. Slowly reaching up, he took hold. The next instant, quick as anything, he was in the saddle with the rope in his hands.

Some of the men whooped.

"Hush, you damned nuisances," Texas Jack yelled louder than they had. "You might spook her or make her mad."

High Eagle jiggled the rope. Myrtle didn't move. He lightly slapped his legs. She didn't move. He jabbed his heels. She didn't move. He looked at Texas Jack and gestured as if to say, "What do I do?"

"Try tickling her ears," Texas Jack hollered. "Females always like that."

"I don't," Mandy said.

High Eagle had to bend to do it. He touched Myrtle's ear and she trembled. He gave her ear a tug, and suddenly she lumbered into motion but as slow as a tortoise.

"Will you look at that," Evans marveled.

"A man riding a buffalo," Stubbs said. "Don't this beat all."

Texas Jack climbed on the fence to watch. "I am so happy, boys, I could cry. This makes me the master of my destiny. I'll own a mansion and have maids in French uniforms." He smirked at Fargo. "What do you have to say now, Mr. Doom-and-Gloom?"

Fargo sighed. "You haven't put on the first show and already you're rich."

"I have vision. I have dreams. I'm a man ahead of his time."

"Gosh," Schumer said.

"What you are," Fargo said, "is full of it."

"Wait and see," Texas Jack said. "We're over the biggest hurdle. Things will go smoothly from here on out." He spread his arms wide and grinned. "Let's get us more buffalo."

27

The new herd was smaller, a few thousand buffs grazing on either side of a stream. Some were lying down. Some rolled in wallows. Most were cows and calves.

Fargo put his hands on his saddle horn and surveyed the legion of hide and horns. "We're pushing our luck."

"There you go again," Texas Jack said. "You always expect the worst." He gulped from his flask and patted his stomach. "One buff isn't enough. To draw in crowds we need more."

"How many?" Calhoun asked.

In addition to the Texan, Travers, Stubbs, Evans, Reese, and the old hunter, Lefty, were along, as well as High Eagle and Running Bear.

"I'd like twenty or thirty but I reckon three or four should do," Texas Jack said.

"You fixin' to train them like you did Myrtle?"

"It worked with her—it'll work with others. Why?"

"We'll need a hell of a lot more whiskey."

"First things first. Ready your ropes, gentlemen." Texas Jack rose in his stirrups. "Let's see. Which one shall we go after first?"

"How about a calf?" Evans suggested. "We rope one, its ma will come along as peaceful as you please."

"You know, that's not a bad idea," Texas Jack said. "And calves are easier to catch."

"The mother might not like it," Fargo warned.

"All these years," Texas Jack said, "I never realized how much of a grump you are. Do you *ever* look at the bright side?" He gigged his horse. "Come on, boys. Let's do this. See that calf yonder, near the edge of the herd? The one that's scampering around its mother? We'll catch him first."

Calhoun brought his horse close to the Ovaro. "For what it's worth, I agree with you. We're askin' for trouble by ropin' a calf."

"Why didn't you say something?"

"What good would it do? Once Jack gets a notion into his noggin, there's no talkin' him out of it."

The buffalo became aware of them; a timbre of agitation rippled among the herd. Those on the ground rose. Older cows converged to protect the rest. Only the calves were oblivious.

Travers was out in front. Loosening his rope and holding the loop against his leg, he suddenly spurred toward the calf that Texas Jack had picked. It was a dozen feet from its mother, who had planted her legs and held her head low.

"Watch out for the ma!" Calhoun hollered.

Travers slowed and his arm rose. He was good with a rope. The loop seemed to hang suspended in the air over the calf, then settled as lightly as a fluttering butterfly and was around the calf's neck. Travers slowed so he wouldn't hurt the calf when he pulled on the rope.

The calf bleated in fear.

Its mother exploded into motion, coming to its rescue. Her heavy hooves pounding, she swept toward her offspring's would-be abductor.

"Get out of there!" Calhoun bawled.

Travers tried. He reined away and was broadside to the cow when she rammed into his chestnut. The horse squealed as the buffalo's twin scythes ripped in and up. Travers tried to push clear of the saddle. He had one leg up when the chestnut crashed down, pinning his other leg underneath.

"Not again," Calhoun said.

Fargo and the others raced to his rescue. Some of the men shouted and yipped, thinking to drive the cow off.

The mother tore at the chestnut in a frenzy, her horns ripping and rending. There was no hope for the horse. Travers was struggling to free his leg and scramble away. The cow saw him. She bounded over the chestnut and brought her front hooves down on his chest.

In spite of the yelling, Fargo heard the *crack* of ribs as they shattered and saw blood spurt from Travers's nose and mouth.

The cow's horns flashed. One hooked Travers's neck and half severed it from his body. The other sliced into a shoulder and nearly tore his arm off.

"Stop her!" Texas Jack cried.

Fargo swung wide. There was no helping Travers. Other buffalo were rushing to the mother's defense and soon there would be a score to deal with. He and the others had to get out of there while they still could.

"I want that calf," Texas Jack bellowed, and galloped toward it.

"Jack, you damned fool," Calhoun shouted.

Fargo swore and reined toward Jack. Another cow was sweeping toward him and Jack didn't see her. Drawing his Colt, Fargo fired two shots into the ground in front of her. The shots had no effect but they did cause Jack to snap his head around and discover his peril. Jack hauled on his reins to flee. His roan was fast but so was the cow. Head down, the cow rammed into the roan's rear legs. The roan went down. So did the cow, their legs entangled.

Texas Jack leaped clear. He rolled and came up on his hands and knees.

Fargo was almost to him. He shoved the Colt into his holster and yelled, "Grab hold." He was focused on Jack and almost didn't spot yet another cow that was bearing down on them.

Fargo had only instants in which to act. He grabbed Texas Jack's arm and swung him up behind him even as he reined sharply aside. The cow hurtled past, her horn missing the Ovaro by inches. Fargo went to bring the stallion to a gallop but another cow was in front of them, her horns poised to thrust. Once more Fargo hauled on the reins. He realized the Ovaro wouldn't turn in time; the cow would slam into the stallion as the other cow had slammed into the chestnut. He clawed for his Colt in a bid to stem the inevitable.

That was when a rifle boomed and part of the cow's head blew off. She pitched into a slide that brought her to a stop almost under the Ovaro's hooves.

"Get the hell out of there," Lefty yelled as he hurriedly replaced the spent cartridge in his smoking Sharps.

Fargo galloped off and looked back. The blast had brought

most of the buffs to a stop. An older cow was thundering toward Stubbs, who was rigid in panic. Again the Sharps mimicked a cannon and the cow crumpled like so much wet wash.

The rest of the herd fled. Cows, calves, bulls, flowed to the south in a grunting, bellowing river of churning limbs and flying tails.

Fargo slowed and turned the Ovaro. It struck him that Texas Jack was being uncommonly quiet. "Are you all right?"

Jack glumly nodded. "He was a good man, Travers. Always did what I asked without griping."

The others had gathered around the body. Calhoun was off his horse and on one knee, his head bowed. "Damn it to hell," he said, and looked at Texas Jack. "This is your fault."

"I know."

"If you hadn't made us—" Calhoun blinked and stopped. "What did you just say?"

"I said I know it's my fault," Texas Jack said. "I was the one who insisted we needed more buffs."

"At least you're man enough to admit it."

"All I could think of was the money we'd make," Texas Jack said.

Fargo couldn't think of a single instance ever when his friend had regretted anything. "What are you trying to pull?"

"Honestly, Skye," Texas Jack said, sliding down. "Must you make a mockery of my good intentions? I tell you, I've come to my senses."

"Hell must be freezing over," Fargo said.

Jack stepped to Travers and stared at the grisly remains. "How can you poke fun at a time like this?" He bent and touched his fingers to the blood on Travers's brow. "See here?" He held his hands so everyone could. "No more, I say. My Extravaganza isn't worth another life. Buffalo are too unpredictable, too dangerous. We'll have to be content with Myrtle."

"Will one buff draw that many people?" Stubbs asked.

"Hard to say," Texas Jack said. "Probably not. Which is why we should give some thought to collecting other animals. What if"—Jack paused and his face lit with either inspiration or greed—"what if we had all kinds? Like that Noah and his ark?"

"How are we supposed to catch them?" a thickset man called Sloane asked.

"We'll come up with a way," Texas Jack said. "I've been pondering this for a few days now, and what the Extravaganza needs is a variety of animals—critters that will give folks a good scare, like Myrtle will."

"I knew it," Fargo said.

"Give us a for instance," Evans said.

"Rattlesnakes, for starters," Texas Jack said. "We dig a small pit and throw them in and let people poke them with a stick for a dollar or two."

"Rattlesnakes shouldn't be hard to catch," Stubbs said. "They're all over."

"What else?" Lefty inquired.

"Scorpions," Texas Jack answered.

"We can do that," Sloane said.

"How about a coyote or two?" Texas Jack proposed. "We rig traps and lure them in with meat. We can do the same with a fox and a bobcat."

"That's an awful lot of critters," Lefty said.

"One more should do it," Texas Jack said. "I've saved the best for last."

"A polecat?" Reese said, and some of them laughed.

"No, not a skunk," Jack said. "An animal that will scare people even more than Myrtle, a beast that none of them have ever set eyes on but that everyone has heard of. I refer, gentlemen, to the true terror of the plains and the mountains."

Calhoun swore. "He can't mean what I think he means."

"Care to bet?" Fargo said.

Texas Jack smiled benignly and raised his hands over his head like a preacher on the stump. "Our Extravaganza won't be complete without it."

"Without *what*?" Lefty said.

"A grizzly."

28

That night the men sat around arguing. Should they or shouldn't they? Most opposed the idea. They agreed with Lefty, who declared, "I ain't going after no griz and I don't care if he fires me over it. I like breathing more than I like being torn to bits."

Texas Jack made the rounds, trying to convince them to change their minds. He was his usual grandiloquent self. "Gentlemen," Fargo heard him say. "A grizzly will bring in people by the thousands. Grizzlies are monsters. Living horrors. They give folks nightmares. We add one to our menagerie and I can guarantee our Extravaganza will be a sensation. Your pokes will bulge with money."

"We can't spend it if we're dead," Stubbs said.

"We'll take precautions," Texas Jack said. "We'll build a cage strong enough to hold ten grizzlies."

"And how do we catch it, boss?" Reese asked. "We can't rope it like we did that buff."

"Why not?"

The looks they gave Jack were almost comical.

"Now we know you're loco," Calhoun said.

"Picture it, boys," Texas Jack said. "A dozen or more of us, swooping down on a griz. It will be so confused, it won't know who to attack. And while it stands there unsure what to do, we throw a dozen ropes around it."

"Boss, don't take this wrong," a man said, "but you need to stay off the bug juice."

"A griz will bite through ropes like we bite through string beans," said another.

"Not only that, I never yet heard of a griz being confused by who or what to kill," Stubbs said.

"Tell you what." Lefty spoke up. "You throw the first rope, boss, and if the griz doesn't kill you, we'll throw ours."

Texas Jack frowned. "Boys, I'm disappointed. I took you for braver men."

"You took us for stupid is what you took us."

"And you ain't takin' us for stupid any longer."

On that irate note Texas Jack sucked on his flask and went to his tent.

"Do you believe that hombre?" Calhoun asked Fargo.

"You never know what to expect with Jack," Fargo said.

It was pushing midnight when Fargo went to his tent. Mandy had drifted off on her own earlier and wasn't there. He didn't think much of it, and turned in. About the middle of the night a sound woke him and he cracked his eyes to see her undressing by her cot. He went back to sleep.

Morning broke cloudy and windy. A storm front was moving in. The tops of the trees bent and the grass rippled like a green ocean.

Fargo was having his second cup of coffee when Texas Jack ambled over and hunkered.

"We need to talk, pard."

"The answer is no."

Jack filled a cup and sipped before saying, "I haven't even said what I want."

"When you do the answer will still be no."

Texas Jack sat back. "I'd like you to circulate and convince the men that it's in their best interests to go along with me on capturing a griz."

"Why don't I just shoot them and save the bear the trouble?"

"It can be done, I tell you."

"Name me one person who ever caught a griz and put it on display," Fargo challenged him.

"We'll be the first."

"I thought so."

Jack placed his elbows on his knees. "Just because something *hasn't* been done doesn't mean it *can't*. Why, if everyone took your attitude, no one would ever do anything."

"You are a piss-poor philosopher."

"Hear me out. There's plenty of timber. We do as I proposed

last night. Build a cage. Set meat as bait. The bear walks in and is caught. No one has to go anywhere near it. No one will be bit or clawed or dead."

"This is a griz we're talking about, Jack. Not a chipmunk."

"There's an idea."

"What is?"

"Chipmunks. We should catch a few. Kids will love them. Maybe a squirrel or a bunny, too."

"Why not wolves and a black bear while we're at it? Hell, catch a brown one and everyone will think it's a griz," Fargo said sarcastically. A lot of people didn't know that black bears weren't always black. They came in shades from cinnamon to brown. Once he saw one that was almost yellow.

Texas Jack gave a start. "My God. You've done it again."

"Done what?"

"That's brilliant. It's exactly what we'll do," Jack said excitedly. "The men aren't scared of black bears. We'll find a brown one and claim it's a young griz and folks back east won't ever know the difference." He clapped Fargo on the arm. "And since it's your brainstorm, it's only fair that you be the one to catch it."

"I should have let Calhoun shoot you," Fargo said.

29

Texas Jack sent the Pawnees out. High Eagle and Running Bear and Lost Toe were gone three days. On the fourth morning High Eagle and Running Bear came galloping into camp to report that they had come across a black bear that wasn't black. Lost Toe was keeping an eye on it.

Jack marshaled the men. Ten riders, plus Fargo, headed west along the Platte River. Running Bear led them. High Eagle said he wasn't feeling well and stayed behind.

The growth along the river was thick and abundant with wildlife. Sparrows chirped and warblers warbled. Pheasants flew and a wood thrush sang. Squirrels ran from tree limb to tree limb and rabbits bounded off in alarm. They saw plenty of does and fawns and a few young bucks.

The men were in good spirits. They didn't mind going after a black bear. Unlike grizzlies, black bears were more likely to run than attack.

Calhoun, Stubbs, Lefty, and Sloane were among those in the party. Calhoun rode beside Fargo.

"Jack says this is the last critter we need," the Texan mentioned. "Then it's off to Saint Louis, and riches."

"I'll believe it when I see the money rolling in," Fargo said.

Calhoun chuckled. "We've got to hand it to him, though. He's a dreamer but he works damn hard to make his dreams come true. And he's not afraid to get his hands dirty. He's been in the thick of it with us."

"I'll give him that," Fargo allowed. He became aware that Calhoun was staring at him and looked over. "Something else on your mind?"

"It's none of my business. But you're takin' it better than I would."

"If I knew what it was, I might tell you why."

"It's your girl," Calhoun said.

Fargo ducked to avoid a low limb. "I didn't know I had one."

"Then who have you been sharin' your tent with? Your sister?" Calhoun grinned good-naturedly. "Word was you were sweet on her, and now that she's taken up with him, well, I reckoned as how you might be a mite put out about it."

"Him who?"

Calhoun swore. "Damn me. I should have kept my mouth shut. It never occurred to me that you didn't know."

"Mandy is a friend," Fargo said. "Nothing more. If she's found a beau, good for her."

"Some of the others don't like it much. They say it ain't fittin', him bein' what he is."

"What is he, exactly?"

"I might as well come out with it," Calhoun said. "Your friend has been keepin' late hours with High Eagle."

Fargo shrugged. "Figures. They're about the same age."

"You don't mind her bein' white and him bein' red?"

"I'd be a damned hypocrite if I did," Fargo said. He'd slept with more than a few Indian women. Lived with a few, too. Strip away the way they were raised and their skin and they were the same as their white sisters. Under the sheets, or a buffalo robe, all women were equal.

"It doesn't bother me none," Calhoun said. "My grandpa took up with an Injun gal after Grandma died. A Comanche, if you can believe it. They lived together pretty near fifteen years."

Fargo recollected some of the Indian maidens he had been with, and smiled.

"Some of the others ain't as forgivin'," Calhoun said. "Stubbs has been makin' noise as how they should take High Eagle off into the woods and beat some respect for white women into him."

"Stubbs?"

"He has a spiteful nature. Enough drink in him and he can be downright mean."

"Thanks for the warning."

"I like that little gal. She's always nice to me. Always wears a smile."

They came to a bend in the river. Beyond, the trees were thick and the belt of grass at the water's edge so high that it came to their mounts' bellies.

Running Bear was in the lead. He turned to Texas Jack and said in English, "This where we see bear. Lost Toe be close."

"How big was this bear?" Texas Jack asked.

"Little," Running Bear said.

"How little?"

Suddenly Running Bear cried out and drew rein and vaulted from his horse. He knelt next to a form sprawled across their path.

Texas Jack raised an arm to bring everyone to a halt and dismounted.

So did Fargo and Calhoun.

"Oh, hell," the real Texan said.

Lost Toe had lost more than his toe. His throat was a ruin and his chest and legs had been clawed to ribbons. Part of his face had been bitten off and three fingers from one hand were lying next to the hand itself.

"No cub did this," Jack said.

"It can't have gotten far," Calhoun said. "Those wounds are fresh."

Just then a dark shape reared in the trees and a roar shattered the stillness.

30

Fargo dropped his hand to his Colt as the biggest black bear he ever laid eyes on lumbered out of the oaks. It was on its hind legs. Or, rather, *she* was. The bear was a female and she had blood on her front paws and rimming her mouth.

Her maw gaped and she sank onto all fours and let out another roar.

Some of the horses reared.

Lefty lunged at his saddle to try to grab his Sharps but his horse ran off before he could pull it from the scabbard.

Running Bear had his bow in his hand and was reaching for his quiver when the bear's claws sheared into his neck. Scarlet sprayed and he toppled.

Fargo fired twice from the hip. Texas Jack got off a shot, too.

The bear recoiled, yowled in pain, then rushed at Sloane's roan. Sloane had drawn his Smith and Wesson and he shot at her head and neck. The black bear's teeth closed on his leg. He screamed as the bear tore his boot from the stirrup and bit through to the bone. There was a *crunch*, and she ripped the bottom of his leg almost all the way off.

Revolvers and rifles banged and boomed. Slugs struck the bear from all sides but they may as well have been drops of rain for all the effect they had.

Sloane was hauled from his saddle. He shrieked as the bear bit at his chest and then his face. There was another *crunch*, and he went silent.

Fargo darted to the Ovaro. He shoved his Colt into his holster and yanked out the Henry. As he turned he levered a round into the chamber. The bear had wheeled toward Texas Jack and Calhoun, both of whom were throwing lead at her as fast as they could shoot. She started toward them and Fargo pressed the Henry's muzzle against her ear and fired. She stumbled and he fired again. Her front legs buckled. He levered another round and jammed the muzzle at her eye and the Henry blasted.

The black bear went down. She was still alive, though, and gnashed at his leg.

Fargo skipped back. He wedged the Henry to his shoulder and put seven more slugs into her body.

A convulsive shake, and the bear was dead.

"Jesus," someone said.

"Look at the Injun."

Even though his head was attached by only a few inches of flesh, Running Bear's body was trembling and twitching.

Calhoun put the muzzle of his Remington to the Pawnee's forehead and squeezed off a shot. The trembling and twitching stopped.

Texas Jack looked at the three bodies and at the body of the bear. "That didn't go well."

"You and your bright ideas," Fargo said.

"Don't blame me. Does that bear look brown to you? Or little? Why in hell did the Pawnees tell us it was?"

From out of the vegetation poked the head of another bear. Ignoring them, it emerged from cover and went up to the female and mewed and licked her.

"I'll be switched," Calhoun said. "She had a cub."

"She was protecting it," Lefty remarked. "That's why she attacked us."

Texas Jack smiled. "And look at what color it is, boys."

The cub was brown, the same brown as many grizzlies. It was eight or nine months old and didn't bristle when Texas Jack stepped up to it and said, "Someone hand me a rope. We have another star for our Extravaganza."

The cub didn't give them a lick of trouble. Lefty was given care of it while the others dug a shallow grave for Sloane. Texas Jack emptied the dead man's pockets and the body was rolled into the hole.

"Now do the Pawnees," Texas Jack said.

"What for?" Stubbs asked.

"They're dead, aren't they?"

Stubbs mopped the sweat on his brow. "They're Injuns. Why go to the bother?"

"They were in my employ, as you are," Texas Jack said. "It's only right we do them the favor."

"But they're redskins," Evans said. "They don't give a hoot about being buried. Hell, some tribes put their dead up on stands."

"I want it done anyway."

Stubbs let go of the branch he had been using to dig with. "No, sir. I won't bury no Injun. I can't hardly stand their kind as it is."

Fargo shoved the Henry into his saddle scabbard and turned. "Bury them."

"We don't work for you," Stubbs said.

"Who do you think you are?" Evans demanded.

Fargo put his hand on his Colt. "I'm the man who won't tell you twice."

Stubbs colored but he picked up the branch and jabbed at the soil. "Fine. We'll bury the lousy savages. But don't think I'll forget this."

"Me either," Evans said.

"Anytime," Fargo told them.

That night Texas Jack called the outfit together and announced that they were leaving for Saint Louis the next day.

"I want to depart by noon," he informed them. "So get a good night's sleep because we'll be up before dawn to get ready."

"This calls for a celebration," Stubbs called out. "Break out the red-eye."

"There will be no drinking until we reach Saint Louis," Texas Jack said. "We're running low and we need what's left to keep Myrtle tamed down."

"Hellfire," a man said. "You let that buff get drunk but not us?"

"What about you, Jack?" Reese hollered. "If we have to give it up, so do you."

"I'm the boss. The rules aren't the same for me as they are for you."

Grumbling and muttering broke out.

Fargo didn't blame them. He could go without if he had to but he'd miss having a cup or two each night before he turned in.

Stubbs turned on Schumer. "This is your fault. You should have brought more whiskey along."

"How was I to know I'd be giving it to a buffalo?" Schumer said. "As it is, I'll have to give her a little less each day until we get there so we don't run out."

"The last thing we want is to have Myrtle be sober," Texas Jack said.

"I still don't like it." Reese wouldn't let it drop.

"Relax and rest tonight," Texas Jack said. "From here on out there'll be a lot of work."

Lefty snickered. "This ain't exactly been a picnic so far."

Fargo went to his tent. He didn't expect Mandy back until late. She had been at the meeting, standing apart from the men. She had been keeping to herself a lot the past few days. Thanks to Calhoun, he knew why.

Fargo sat on his cot. He had no reason to stay up late. He went to tug off a boot.

Spurs jingled outside and someone smacked the flap.

"It's me," Calhoun said.

"I'm turning in," Fargo told him.

"You might want to hold off. There's trouble brewin'. It involves your lady friend."

Fargo pulled his pants leg down and stepped to the flap. "What kind of trouble?"

"I saw her and that young Pawnee go off into the woods."

"She's a grown woman. She can do as she pleases."

"It's not that," Calhoun said. "I wasn't the only one who saw them. So did Stubbs. He and a couple of others went slinkin' off after them."

"Show me where."

The north side of the camp was bordered by dense growth that bordered the Platte. Most of their water came from the river, and over the days and weeks that Texas Jack's company had been there, a trail had been worn down. It passed through a stand of cottonwoods and skirted briars to end at the river's edge.

The sky was moonless, the dark relieved by pale starlight.

Out on the prairie coyotes keened while in the woods an owl hooted.

Fargo was in the cottonwoods when he heard voices. He was almost past the briars when there was a a slap. Mandy said something in anger, and Stubbs laughed. Fargo slowed so as not to give himself away.

High Eagle was on the ground, his arms and legs pinned by Evans and another man called Carver.

Mandy had her back to the river and her fists balled and was glaring at Stubbs. "Lay a finger on me again and I'll slap you harder."

"You little bitch," Stubbs snarled. "Or should I say, you little whore. That's what you are, you know. That's what any white gal is who'd let an Injun do what he was doing."

"Don't you dare hit him again or I'll go to Texas Jack and he'll fire you."

"Maybe he will and maybe he won't. But it'll be worth it to teach this buck not to molest white women."

"He wasn't molesting me," Mandy said. "I brought him here of my own accord."

"Have you no decency?" Stubbs said. "Have you no shame?"

"Leave us be."

"After we've beaten the tar out of him."

"No, please."

Fargo had heard enough. He sidled to the right so he had a clear shot at all three and declared, "That's enough."

Stubbs spun.

Evans straightened and stepped to one side.

Carver pressed his knee to High Eagle's chest to keep him from rising and said, "You just lie there, buck."

"Your gal has been trifling with your affections, mister," Stubbs said. "She's been sneaking off with that red cur. We caught them in the act."

"Let him up," Fargo said.

"Didn't you hear me? We're on your side. I say we beat the Pawnee black-and-blue."

"They can do as they please," Fargo said.

Stubbs gestured. "What are you, an Injun lover?"

"Don't you remember?" Evans said. "He was the one who made us bury those other two."

"That's right," Stubbs said, nodding. "You *are* an Injun lover."

"I can't think of anything I hate more," Carver said.

"Me either."

Carver let go of High Eagle. "How about if the three of us pound some sense into him?"

Stubbs made a fist and hit his other palm, and grinned. "We can pound him and the redskin, both."

"If you're smart," Fargo said, "you'll walk away."

"Listen to him?" Stubbs scoffed.

Calhoun had held back but now he strode forward and said, "I'm with Fargo in this. Back off before someone gets hurt."

"No," Fargo said. "They're mine."

"You hear him?" Stubbs said, and laughed. "Let's stomp the red-loving bastard."

31

Fargo didn't wait for them to come to him. He crossed to them.

Evans had both fists cocked. "We're going to take you down a peg, big man," he said, and threw a looping right.

Fargo blocked and countered with a jab to the chin that rocked Evans on his heels and then a blow to the gut that doubled Evans in half. He swept his knee into Evans's face, felt the nose give, and clubbed Evans behind the ear. Evans fell like an empty sack.

Carver was bigger and brawnier and smarter. He came in slow, balanced on the balls of his feet, a big fist raised to protect his face, his arms protecting his stomach. "I won't be as easy."

Fargo feinted, unleashed a left cross, had it countered. He avoided a straight arm at his jaw and planted a solid punch to Carver's ribs. Carver grunted, shifted, and drove a fist into Fargo's. The pain made Fargo grit his teeth. He dodged an uppercut, connected to Carver's cheek. The cheek split and blood trickled.

Surprisingly, Carver grinned. "Not bad. But I ain't ever been beat with fists and I don't reckon to be beat now."

Fargo had a fight on his hands. They traded a flurry that did little harm to either. Circling, each sought an opening.

Carver tried a hook. Fargo evaded it.

"We could be at this all night," Carver said.

Not if Fargo could help it. Taking a step, he brought his boot down on Carver's toes. Carver cursed and backpedaled and Fargo kicked him in the knee. Carver's leg folded. An uppercut sprawled him flat.

Fargo faced Stubbs. "Now it's just you and me."

Stubbs thrust his palms out. "Hold on. I've changed my mind."

"Too late," Fargo said.

Mandy was suddenly beside Stubbs and reaching for his arm. "Let me," she said. Gripping Stubbs's wrist, she pivoted, flung her foot behind his legs to trip him, and slung him at the river.

Stubbs tried to stop and couldn't. He fell face-first with a splash.

"That's showin' him, girl," Calhoun said.

Stubbs rose sputtering. The water wasn't deep and he came out on his hands and knees, coughing and wheezing. "Damn you. You'll pay for that, you hear?"

By then Fargo had reached him. He palmed his Colt and slashed down, hard. Stubbs looked up just as the barrel connected, and went limp.

"Do it again," Mandy said. "Pistol-whip him until his brains leak out."

High Eagle was trying to stand, a hand to his temple. Fargo reached to steady him but the young Pawnee slapped his hand away.

"No! Not want white man's help."

Mandy slipped her arm around him, saying, "That's no way to be. He helped us."

"They beat me," High Eagle said. Drops of blood were trickling down his face.

"Skye didn't. Be nice to him."

"They white. Him white."

"What kind of logic is that?" Mandy said. "*I'm* white, in case you've forgotten."

Fargo stepped over Evans and around Carver and on up the trail.

"That pup wasn't very grateful," Calhoun said.

"He's her problem."

"I reckon so. Strange, though, him takin' up with her. I thought there was a Pawnee gal he was fond of."

"He's her problem," Fargo said again.

"You have three of your own now. They won't let it rest. When you least expect, they'll jump you."

"Once we get to Saint Louis I'm going my own way." Fargo couldn't wait to be shed of the lunacy.

"And miss the wonders Texas Jack has cooked up?"

"He's had another brainstorm?"

"A whole batch. He's decided that Myrtle and Tiberius ain't enough—"

"Who?"

"That's what Jack is callin' the bear. Tiberius, the Grizzly Terror, or some such."

"It's a damn cub."

"Jack has whipped up a story about how he saved Tiberius from a pack of starvin' wolves and now it dotes over him."

"That's Jack," Fargo said.

"You ain't heard the half of it. You know about those bull-fights they have down to Mexico and over in Spain? Where a gent in fancy clothes flaps a red cape in front of a bull to make the bull attack him?"

"I've heard of them," Fargo said.

"Well, Jack thinks that ridin' Myrtle ain't enough of a spectacle. He wants to use her like they do those bulls."

Fargo stopped so abruptly that Calhoun nearly walked into him. "He wasn't serious?"

"This is Texas Jack we're talkin' about," Calhoun said. "He says that if bullfighting is good enough for those folks, think of how much people will pay to see the first-ever buffalo fighting in all creation."

"He'll be killed."

"Oh, he's not doin' the fightin'. He's dumb but he's not *that* dumb. He has someone else in mind to flap the blanket in the buff's face."

"Who?"

Calhoun grinned.

"Son of a bitch," Fargo said.

32

Texas Jack was perched on the end of his bed, sucking on his flask. He smacked his lips and patted the flask and said, "What do we need water for when we have this?"

"Buffalo fighting?" Fargo said.

"Oh. Someone let the cat out of the bag. Is that why you barged in on me?" Jack laughed and offered the flask. "Have some elixir."

"You couldn't pay me enough."

"All I ask is that you consider it."

"No."

"The public will love it. You'll be famous."

"I'm already too well known as it is," Fargo said. Thanks to a shooting match he'd taken part in with other top shooters and an occasional incident here and there, the newspapers wrote about him more than he liked.

"No one has ever done it before."

"No one has ever jumped off Pike's Peak, either."

Texas Jack sipped and sighed and leaned back. "Have a seat, hoss, and we'll hash this out."

"I've already made up my mind," Fargo said, but he roosted on a folding stool.

"I need you with me," Texas Jack said. "The reason I sent for you is because you're the one person in this whole world I can trust. With my life, if it came to that."

"Don't remind me."

"Remember how we used to sit around playing cards and talk about how we'd like to be rich?"

"We were half drunk half the time."

"So? That doesn't mean we were talking out our asses. I'd

like to have money. My Extravaganza is the answer. It's the best idea I've ever had."

That wasn't saying a lot, Fargo almost said.

"I'll cut you in for a percentage. All I ask is that you help me."

"I came, didn't I?"

"That you did. And after all the work we put in, you shouldn't squawk about playing matador. You flap the blanket a few times and the act is over."

"Find someone else."

Texas Jack tilted his flask. After he lowered it he said, "I expected better of you. We've been pards a long time."

"Don't play that card."

Jack took off his hat and set it on the bed. "You sure can be a stubborn cuss. How about I cut you for it?"

Fargo stared.

Jack got up and went to a pair of saddlebags lying on the ground. He opened a flap and rummaged and held up a pack of cards. "Are you game?"

"You're drunk."

"Hell, I'm always drunk." Jack grinned and sat back down. He riffled the deck, then shuffled several times and set the deck on the cot. "You first. If I get high card, you do the buffalo fighting. If you get high card, I'll do it. That's fair, isn't it?"

"Jack, Jack, Jack."

"Humor me. I asked the Pawnee but all he'll do is ride her."

"He has more sense than you do."

"Cut, please."

Fargo reached over and placed his fingers about a third of the way down and showed the bottom card. It was the seven of hearts.

Texas Jack laughed. "If I can't beat that, I deserve to be gored." He cut and turned the cards over. He had a two of spades. "I'll be damned."

"You're not really going to do it?"

"I said I would."

"The buff will kill you."

"Myrtle will be so drunk, she'll think there are three or four of me. Odds are she'll miss."

Fargo repressed an urge to grab him and shake him until his teeth rattled. "You must have a death wish."

Jack gave his flask a light shake and peered into it. "Hell. I'm getting low. And no, pard. I happen to love life. Not as much as I love whiskey but I wouldn't get to drink if I was dead. I feel most alive when I'm doing things that excite me, like organizing the world's first-ever Frontier Extravaganza."

"Or buffalo fighting."

"And grizzly wrestling."

"And what?"

"That's my other new idea," Texas Jack revealed. "We muzzle the cub and I wrestle it. Everyone will think I'm wrestling a real griz. So what if it's young. They'll still think I'm in danger." He laughed and slapped his leg. "There are days when my brain dazzles me."

Fargo stood.

"Nothing more to say?"

"I hope the cub claws your balls off."

33

Shortly after noon they got under way. Myrtle was plied with whiskey and as meek as a kitten. The black bear cub was in a cage in a wagon, sleeping. The smaller animals were in cages of their own.

The plan was to follow the Platte to civilization and then on to Saint Louis.

Outriders were posted. Texas Jack wasn't taking any chances. They were on the margins of Sioux territory and hostiles might pay them a visit.

Fargo rode with Calhoun. Mandy had let him know the night before that she would be riding with High Eagle. She'd thanked him for saving her life and pecked him on the cheek and walked out of the tent.

Calhoun didn't bring her up. The Texan had more sense. He did mention something else, though, shortly after their caravan got under way. "There's a rumor goin' around. You'd best watch your back, hoss. Stubbs and his pards didn't take kindly to bein' bloodied."

"They're welcome to try," Fargo said. The next time, he wouldn't go so easy on them.

"I aim to stick close and watch your back, if you have no objection."

"I'm obliged," Fargo said.

"You'd do to ride the river with, and I don't say that often."

Fargo grinned and nodded at the Platte. "Good thing we are, then."

"They won't do it straight up," Calhoun warned. "They tried that and you beat the stuffin' out of all three."

Fargo wasn't overly concerned. A lot of times nothing ever came of tough talk. Men did it to let off steam.

"You could prod them," Calhoun suggested. "None of those three is a gun hand and I hear you're mighty slick with that Colt of yours."

"We need them at the moment."

"In case the Sioux attack? I reckon every hombre counts but none of the rest of us will shed tears if you take me up on it."

The day proved uneventful. Night found them camped under a host of stars. Out on the prairie the ever-present coyotes cried and once the screech of a prowling cougar sent a ripple of nerves through the horse string.

Fargo played cards with Texas Jack and Calhoun and a few others until near midnight. The camp was quiet as he made his way to his tent. He opened the flap and stepped into pitch black. Rather than bother with the lantern, he moved to the cot. Careful not to bump his shins, he sat and pulled off his boots. He unbuckled his gun belt and set it next to him. Sleep claimed him almost instantly.

How much time had gone by when his eyes opened was hard to say. He was on his side, facing the flap. He had a vague sense that a noise woke him. He listened but heard only the coyotes and a frog croak along the river. He was about to close his eyes when he realized the flap was partway open. He had tied it when he came in.

Someone was in the tent with him.

Fargo lay still. His hand was inches from the Colt. Whoever it was would have to cross toward him and he could draw and shoot, if need be, in the blink of an eye. He concentrated on the corners where it was blackest and almost missed movement close to the cot. Whoever it was had slunk along the side of the tent and now was right on top of him.

Fargo inched his hand toward his revolver.

A figure loomed and metal glinted dully.

A knife blade, Fargo reckoned.

The assassin crept nearer.

Fargo saw a leg, gauged where the knee was, and slammed his foot against it. The man cried out. Fargo jerked back as the knife speared the cot where his neck had been. He backhanded a fist across his assailant's face and thrust with both legs. The man went stumbling.

Fargo grabbed for his Colt but the holster wasn't there. It had fallen off the cot. He heaved erect. The man was coming at him again and although he couldn't see the figure's face clearly he knew who it was. "Carver," he said.

"Damn right, Injun lover."

"Leave, now, and I'll let you live," Fargo stalled as he groped with his feet for his holster.

"You'll *let* me? Who the hell do you think you are?"

Fargo's left foot bumped something. It had to be the holster. Before he could snatch it up, Carver was on him.

The knife sheared at his chest. He sidestepped and landed a punch to the jaw but in doing so his foot caught on the holster and he tripped.

The next moment he was on the ground with Carver rearing over him.

"I've got you now, you son of a bitch."

34

The knife flashed at Fargo's chest. He flung his arm out and caught hold of Carver's wrist. A knee slammed him in the gut and he retaliated with a blow to the jaw. Carver seized his wrist, and locked together, they grappled. They collided with the cot and it tipped. The knife pricked Fargo's cheek. Exerting all his strength, he heaved Carver off and scrambled into a crouch.

Carver swore and was at him again. Fargo got his hands down and blocked a low thrust. He rammed his fist against Carver's knee.

Carver cursed and slashed. Fargo felt a sting on his left arm. He unleashed an uppercut that lifted Carver onto his toes. He swung again, smashing Carver back. His left foot bumped something: his gun belt. Dropping, Fargo scooped the Colt out. He fired as Carver came at him, fired as Carver raised the knife, fired as Carver collapsed.

Fargo slowly stood. He was sore and his arm was bleeding. He went to the flap and pushed it open and heard footsteps pound away into the night. Someone had stood lookout. Stubbs or Evans, Fargo reckoned, fleeing before the gunshots brought others.

The night filled with moving shadows. Men came from all over, some pulling on shirts or strapping on gun belts. Several bore lanterns.

Texas Jack barreled from among them. "Was that you doing the shooting?"

Fargo motioned for Jack to go in the tent, and stepped aside.

More arrived, among them Calhoun. Questions were thrown at Fargo but the only one he answered was the Texan's.

"They tried, didn't they?"

"Carver," Fargo said.

"Damn. And I promised to watch your back."

The flap bulged and Jack came out. "Mind telling me what this was all about?"

Fargo kept it short. When he was done, Calhoun chimed in that he had been a witness to the fight at the river.

Texas Jack surveyed the company. "Where are Stubbs and Evans? I don't see them anywhere."

"We're here," Stubbs said, and came around the side of Fargo's tent with Evans at his side.

"You heard Fargo just now?" Texas Jack said.

"I heard his pack of lies," Stubbs said. "Sure, we had a disagreement. But we weren't out to hurt the Pawnee. All we wanted was to scare him some."

"I won't stand for that kind of behavior," Texas Jack said. "And kindly explain why your friend tried to commit murder."

"We had nothing to do with that."

"Liar," Calhoun muttered.

"Carver was mad about being made to look the fool," Stubbs said. "He couldn't let it drop like Evans and me."

"Did Carver tell you he was going to come after Fargo?"

"No, or I'd have let you know."

"We're supposed to believe that?" Calhoun asked.

"Stay out of this," Stubbs said.

Fargo stepped up to him and before Stubbs could guess what he was up to, he pressed the Colt's muzzle against Stubbs's forehead. "Are you paying attention?"

Stubbs swallowed and said, "I'm telling the truth, damn your hide."

"If you or your pard make more trouble, both of you die."

"Hey now," Evans said. "What did I do?"

"Did you hear him?" Stubbs said to Texas Jack. "He just threatened us."

"I heard."

"What are you going to do bout it?"

"Not a blessed thing."

"You're taking his side?"

"I've known Skye a lot longer than I have you," Texas

Jack said. "I'd take his word over anyone's. But it could be you're telling the truth and didn't have a hand in Carver trying to kill him. So I won't have you tossed out on your ears."

"If you weren't so partial you'd toss him out."

Texas Jack poked Stubbs in the chest. "*You* started it by beating up High Eagle. I'm surprised he didn't come to me and—" Jack looked around again. "Where is he, anyhow? And Mandy, too?"

"Off in the woods," someone said.

Texas Jack tiredly rubbed his eyes. "We have a body to plant. Stubbs, Evans, the job is yours."

"Why us?" Stubbs said.

"Because I said so."

"God, you are high-handed."

"He was your friend. The rest of you, back to your blankets." Texas Jack walked off.

Stubbs and Evans entered Fargo's tent, Stubbs grumbling, "Who does he think he is?"

Calhoun nudged Fargo and said quietly, "This isn't the end of it. You know that, don't you?"

"I know," Fargo said.

35

The company had been under way an hour. Fargo was riding ahead of the wagons when hooves thudded and Mandy slowed next to him. Her hair was swept back and tied and her cheeks were pink with the flush of youth, and something else.

"Morning."

"Howdy, stranger," Fargo said.

"I thought we should talk. I figured I owed you that much, you having saved me from the Sioux, and all."

"You don't owe me a thing."

"You're not mad?"

"About what?"

"You know."

Fargo looked at her. "If you mean your new beau, what would I be mad about? You're not my wife. You're not my true love. You were fun and it was nice but there's nothing more."

"Oh my. I suppose I deserved that."

"Damn it, girl," Fargo said in annoyance. "You don't *deserve* anything. All I'm saying is that I didn't have any hold on you and you sure as hell didn't have any on me."

"You're awful blunt."

"Want me to sugarcoat it? Want me to say I'll always hold you special in my heart? That I'd scribble poems about you and cry over you at night and miss you until the end of my days?"

Mandy snorted, then laughed. "I see your point. Sorry I made more out of what I've done than there is."

"There you go again. Stop apologizing. Live how you want and the rest of the world be damned."

"Well, then," Mandy said, "I should still explain."

"No need."

"Yes, there is," Mandy persisted. "It happened all of a sudden. We went for walks and talked and before I knew it, I had feelings for him. We have a lot in common, High Eagle and me."

"Pawnees and farm girls usually do."

"Now you're being sarcastic. Not our backgrounds but what we want out of life."

"What would that be?"

"Good things. Good clothes. A good place to live. I really didn't think about it much until lately, but now that I've been thrown on my own and see how hard life can be, I want it any way I can get it."

"Good luck."

"Luck isn't always enough. A person has to reach out and take what they want and not let anyone stop them. I aim to do just that."

"Where does your new lover fit in?"

Mandy coughed. "He wants the same things. A better life for himself. It's why he learned English, why he joined up with Texas Jack. He's looking for the golden ring."

"Most Pawnees are content to live as their people have for ages."

"Not High Eagle. He's different. He has ambition. More than me, maybe."

"Watch yourself when we get to Saint Louis," Fargo advised.

"In what regard?"

"A lot of folks feel the same as Stubbs and his friends. They don't like red and white to mix. Ladies will turn their noses up at you and some of the men will want to beat him, or worse."

"It's none of their business."

"When has that ever stopped busybodies? Or bigots? Or, hell, anyone?" Fargo shook his head. "People never let common sense get in the way of their hate."

"Thanks for the warning. And yes, we'll be careful. If things go well, our stay in Saint Louis will be fairly short."

"Oh?"

Mandy looked off across the prairie and they rode in silence for a while until she said, "Life sure is strange. If someone had told me six months ago that one day I'd be doing what I am doing, I'd have said they were crazy."

Fargo liked it that way. He liked never knowing what the next day would bring. To him, the life of a store clerk or a banker, doing the same day in and day out, would be living hell.

"How long are you fixing to stay with Texas Jack?"

"I was going to light a shuck as soon as we get to Saint Louis," Fargo confessed, "but now I reckon I'll stick around and watch him kill himself buffalo fighting."

"I heard about that. I thought it was a joke."

"Jack's whole life is a joke," Fargo said. "He just doesn't know it."

"Yet you came when he said he needed you."

"Just because a friend is a jackass doesn't make him less of a friend."

Mandy giggled. "I'm happy you're not mad at me. I hope you continue not to be."

"Why wouldn't I?"

"Tell me something. Have *you* ever hankered after the finer things in life? Ever wanted more money than you'd know what to do with?"

Fargo shrugged. "I don't lose sleep over it."

"Being thrown on my own has opened my eyes. I was naive. But not anymore. When we reach Saint Louis, it will be root hog or die." Mandy smiled. "If it lands me in an early grave, so be it. Who wants to live forever?" She reined around and trotted back down the line to rejoin High Eagle.

Fargo twisted in the saddle and stared after her. He didn't like the sound of that.

36

Saint Louis was booming. From all over people were flocking to the gateway to the West. Jobs were plentiful, thanks to the flood of goods and emigrants that flowed through the city. The population was more than one hundred and fifty thousand and climbing.

Steamboats clogged the Mississippi River. Saloons, grog shops, and taverns peppered the waterfront. Higher up, wealth and culture were on display. Limestone mansions gleamed in the sunlight. There were several newspapers, two bookstores, and luxurious theaters.

After the stark savagery of the wilds, it was a whole new world.

Fargo rode in with Texas Jack. Jack had on his best buckskins and had polished his boots and wore a long white silk bandanna that he jauntily draped over his shoulder. He had on spotless white gauntlets, too.

"Where in blazes did you get those?" Fargo asked.

"From my trunk." Texas Jack smiled and waved at passersby who had stopped to stare. "Look at them. We'll be the talk of the city."

Jack wasn't the only attraction. The canvas had been taken down from the first wagon so everyone could see the cage with Tiberius. And then there was Myrtle. Calhoun and four others hemmed her in case she acted up. So far she hadn't. But then, they had given her so much whiskey right before entering the city that she was in a dazed stupor. The general hubbub had no effect.

Texas Jack winked at a pretty woman twirling a pink parasol. "I'll be so famous, women will climb over themselves to have me."

"If you say so."

"Don't doubt me. I've been right about everything else, haven't I?"

"Usually when you're right," Fargo said, "it's by accident."

"Hardy-har-har," Jack said, and flourished his hat at a pair of women in tight dresses.

"Where are we putting up for the night?" Fargo wondered. They had about two hours of daylight left.

"Don't you worry," Texas Jack said. "I worked it out before I left."

A man separated from the onlookers and barred their way. He wore a high round hat and a uniform with large buttons that ran from his neck to his waist. He also had a night stick that he smacked against his palm. "What's this, then?" he demanded.

Fargo drew rein.

"Good afternoon, Officer," Texas Jack greeted him. "You happen to be looking on Texas Jack Lavender's Great Frontier Extravaganza."

"Lavender?" the policeman repeated. "Would you be the same gentleman who got drunk last New Year's and went along Terry Street shooting out streetlamps and windows?"

"You did what?" Fargo said.

"That's quite a memory you have there, Officer." Texas Jack laughed. "I was a mite frisky that night. But I paid my fine and was released."

"I'm Officer O'Grady, and I'd like to know what all those animals are here for."

"Why, they're part of the show," Texas Jack said. "We'll have raging buffalo and roaring grizzlies. Bring the wife and the kids." He went to gig his mount.

"Hold on, there." Officer O'Grady peered past Jack's horse at the wagons and the menagerie. "I don't know as I can permit this."

"Why in God's name not?"

"I'm sure there's an ordinance against bringing dangerous animals into the city."

"Dangerous?" Texas Jack scoffed.

"You just said you have raging buffalo. I heard you with my own ears."

"Well, yes, that's what we'll print on our posters to bring in the crowds." Texas Jack gestured. "But look at Myrtle. As you can plainly see, she's as tame as a kitten."

"Myrtle? What kind of name is that for a buffalo?"

"The bear is called Tiberius," Fargo said.

Officer O'Grady looked at him as if he wasn't quite sane. "I'll have to ask you to wait here while I consult with my superiors."

"At least allow us to go on to Councilman Floyd's," Texas Jack said. "He's agreed to put us up at his farm south of here."

"You should have gone directly there, then, and not come parading down Main Street."

"That's the whole purpose," Texas Jack said. "To advertise our presence."

Officer O'Grady took note of the swelling number of onlookers and the commotion the caravan was creating, and frowned. "Very well. I can't have you congesting traffic." He wagged his night stick at Texas Jack. "But mark my words. If your kitten of a buffalo rampages, or any of your other animals cause damage or harm, you'll be held accountable."

"Don't you worry," Texas Jack assured him. "I have everything under control."

37

At one time, before Saint Louis's population swelled, Councilman Floyd's farm had been outside the city limits. Now it was fifty acres of green surrounded by buildings and streets. The value of the land had gone up and was still rising, which was why the councilman hadn't sold it.

As they were dismounting, the councilman came out of the farmhouse. An older man with heavy jowls, he warmly embraced Texas Jack. "Jack! Jack! You're back safe and sound. But I'd expect no less from the greatest scout there is, ever was, or ever will be."

"My blushes, sir," Texas Jack said modestly.

"Do you even know how?" Fargo said.

Councilman Floyd clapped Jack on the back. "This man is a marvel, I tell you. We met years ago. He guided me on a hunt on the plains, and I've never been so impressed by another human being in my life."

"What did he do to impress you?" Fargo asked.

"Rather ask me what he *didn't* do," Floyd said. "He saved us from a prairie fire that nearly burned us all to death. He drove off a horde of hostiles with a single pistol shot. And as for his tracking skills, is there another man alive who can track an ant across solid rock?"

"Now, now," Texas Jack said. "We don't want to bore Fargo with my exploits."

"Fargo? Skye Fargo?" Councilman Floyd said. "You have some scouting ability yourself, I hear. It must be wonderful to be able to learn from a master like Texas Jack."

"It gets more wonderful by the day," Fargo said.

Councilman Floyd gazed past them and stiffened. "Why, is that a buffalo I see?"

"A tame one," Texas Jack said.

"My God, man. You've tamed one of the brutes? Is there nothing you can't do?" Without waiting for an answer, the councilman hustled toward Myrtle.

Fargo stared at Texas Jack.

"What?"

Fargo kept on staring.

"I might have laid it on a little thick," Jack said. "I wanted to impress him so he would recommend me to his friends."

"The ant?"

"I had it wrapped in a handkerchief in my pocket. I pretended to come across its sign and to track it and slipped it out of my pocket and put it on the rock."

"The prairie fire?"

"I set it myself. Had my men wet the grass first so it gave off a lot a smoke and seemed bigger than it was."

"The horde of hostiles?"

"A couple of my men dressed as Injuns. It was an hour or so before dawn, so the councilman couldn't tell how many there were."

"Have you walked on water yet?"

"I have to make a living the same as everybody else. Guided hunts are big money. So what if I add a little excitement? Nobody was hurt."

"You are the greatest," Fargo said dryly.

They strolled over to where Calhoun and Lefty were placing Myrtle in a corral attached to the barn.

Councilman Floyd was agog. "I've never seen the like. I looked into that buffalo's eyes and I would swear it's as harmless as a puppy. How did you do it?"

Texas Jack tapped his temple. "By the power of the mind, sir. Remember, the Good Book says that the Good Lord gave us dominion over the animals."

"You control that buffalo through the force of your will? My word," Councilman Floyd exclaimed. "You must have the greatest brain on the planet."

"God help us," Fargo said.

Texas Jack glanced sharply at him, then smiled and draped an arm around the councilman. "I need your advice, Artemis.

Is there a printer you can recommend? I have to print flyers for our Extravaganza."

"Where are you going to hold it?" Floyd asked.

"I was hoping," Jack said, motioning, "that you would consent to have it here. My men can build an arena at the other end of the corral. It would mean tearing up your soybeans, though, and I'm reluctant to ask you to make that sacrifice."

"Nonsense," Councilman Floyd said. "What are a few soybeans when I get to see your genius at work."

"Do you know where I can get some wood cheap for the fencing?"

"My good friend Councilman Deever can help there. For free seats he'll cut you a deal. I'll talk to him personally and impress on him that helping you is a boon to humanity."

"I have a question," Fargo interrupted.

"Why, of course, my good fellow. What can I do for you?"

"Where's the nearest saloon?"

38

It took five days to build the "arena," as Texas Jack called it: a three-rail fence that encircled several acres and connected to stands for seating.

Fargo had little to do. He'd have been damned if he'd help build the fence. He saw little of Mandy and spent most of his time at Hauk's Saloon. The former river rat who owned it didn't water down the whiskey and ran honest poker tables. Fargo fell back on his second profession, gambling, and by the time the arena was done, he was three hundred and forty-one dollars to the better.

Posters were posted all over the city. The first Extravaganza was to take place on a Saturday afternoon. Tickets were a dollar for those along the fence and four dollars for a seat in the stands.

Fargo was drinking coffee with Texas Jack in the kitchen of the farmhouse when the townsman Jack had hired to oversee ticket sales bustled in.

"I thought you would want to know, Mr. Lavender. We have sold out the first two shows and have half the tickets for the third sold, as well."

Jack grinned at Fargo. "What did I tell you? Money hand over fist."

"It appears you'll average about twenty-five hundred dollars a performance."

"With three performances a week, that's—" Jack's brow puckered.

"Thirty thousand dollars a month, sir."

"I *am* a genius," Jack said. "From here we'll go on to New Orleans and other cities. Within a year I'll have made—" His forehead puckered again.

"Over three hundred and fifty thousand dollars, sir, after expenses, of course."

Fargo whistled. That *was* a lot of money. "You're on your way to being rich."

"Don't jinx it. I don't have the money yet." Texas Jack regarded the bearer of the good tidings. "I'm obliged, Thackery. Is the money being kept at the office, like I said?"

"Yes, sir," Thackery confirmed.

The "office" was a shack next to the stands. Fargo had been in it only once. There were a desk and a chair and a chest for the money and that was it.

"That'll be all, then."

"Yes, sir."

"I'll give you your cut after the first show," Jack said to Fargo.

"I trust you." The irony of it was, Fargo did. Jack had his share of less than sterling traits but he never cheated a friend.

A shaft of sunlight spilled into the kitchen from the sun, which hung low on the horizon.

Fargo pushed back his chair. "I'm off to Hauk's." If he wasn't there early enough he'd have to wait for a seat at the poker tables to empty.

"I'd join you but I still have a lot to do to get ready."

Jack pulled out his flask.

Fargo walked to the saloon. It was only a quarter of a mile and he could use the exercise. The sun was almost down by the time he got there and the streets were mired in shadow. He pushed through the batwings and over to the bar and slapped it to get the bartender's attention.

"The usual?"

Fargo nodded, and when the whiskey came, he raised the glass to his lips and slowly sipped.

Two poker games were under way. Debating which to join, Fargo idly glanced at the wall-length mirror. At a far corner table sat a man with his hat pulled low and his chin tucked to his chest. A bottle was in front of him. He could have passed for just another drinker, except that Fargo knew who he was and suspected why he was hiding his face.

"Well, now," Fargo said to the empty air. He checked every other man in the place but didn't recognize any of them.

So was it coincidence? he asked himself. Or was he right to be suspicious?

A chair opened and Fargo sat in on a game. The three townsmen already at the table were poor players. Their expressions gave too much away; apparently they had never heard of a poker face. Fargo was sixty dollars ahead by ten o'clock. He hated to quit while he was on a winning streak.

The man at the corner table had turned toward him earlier and watched him the whole time from under the lowered hat brim.

It was good the man was so obvious, Fargo reflected. Otherwise he might have gotten a knife in the back or a bullet in the back of his head. Or maybe the man only wanted to beat him black-and-blue.

Fargo raked in his winnings and announced he was done. He stuffed the money into his poke, the poke into a pocket, and pushed back his chair. He made a show of stretching and yawning and ambled to the batwings. In the mirror, the man at the far table stood.

Fargo smiled to himself and went out. The street was dark, save for islands of light from occasional lamps. He turned left and strolled along as if he didn't have a care in the world until he came to a narrow alley between high buildings. Quickly darting into it, he slid his hand under his shirt and palmed his Colt. His gun belt was in his tent at the farm; Saint Louis had an ordinance against wearing firearms.

Boots clomped on the boardwalk and someone started to pass the alley.

Grabbing the stalker's arm, Fargo shoved him against a wall and jammed the Colt against his ribs. "Are you looking for me, Evans?"

Evans did a strange thing. He smiled. "What do you think you're doin'?" he asked as calmly as if they were shaking hands and there wasn't a six-shooter pressed against his side.

"I don't like being followed."

"Why would I follow you? I just had a few drinks and I'm on my way back to the farm."

Fargo didn't believe him but he didn't have proof, only his suspicion. He stepped back. "You get one warning. The next time I won't go easy."

"There won't be a next time," Evans said.

"That's good to hear."

"Not so good for you," said a voice behind Fargo, and a gun muzzle gouged the back of his neck.

39

"Remember me?" Stubbs said, and reaching around, he relieved Fargo of the Colt.

Evans drew his six-shooter. "Let's do it and get it over with."

"Not so fast," Stubbs said. He shoved Fargo deeper into the alley. "Keep walking until I tell you to stop."

Fargo complied. He'd blundered, badly. He should have realized Stubbs was around somewhere.

The alley was so narrow that they had to walk in single file. That gave Fargo an idea. To distract them he said, "You waited long enough."

"I'd wait until hell froze over for another chance at you," Stubbs said. "No one pistol-whips me and gets away with it."

"What now?" Fargo fished for their intent. "You pistol-whip me?"

"You wish that was all."

"What's that?" Evans said. "Beat him and rob him. That's what you told me."

"Jackass," Stubbs replied. "And have him come after us? You want that?"

"But the other," Evans said.

"Quit your whining." Stubbs jabbed Fargo between the shoulder blades. "That's far enough. Turn around. I want to see your eyes when I do it."

Fargo stopped and turned, his arms in the air. The muzzle was six inches from his face. "People will hear the shot. They'll come running."

"He's right," Evans said. "We'll be seen. I'm not hankerin' to end my days with a noose around my neck."

"Damn it, use your head," Stubbs said. "It's too dark for

anyone to get a good look at us and we'll be long gone before the law comes."

"I don't like it," Evans said.

"You're turning yellow. But if it will shut you up, hand me that pigsticker of yours. We'll do it quiet."

"I hope I don't regret this," Evans said, and passed a long-bladed knife over Stubbs's shoulder, hilt first.

Fargo was ready. When Stubbs took his eyes off him to reach for the knife, he slammed a boot against Stubbs's knee. Stubbs cried out and staggered. Fargo clamped his hand on Stubbs's wrist to keep him from using the six-shooter and drove a fist at Stubbs's belly.

Stubbs swore and tried to bury the knife.

Fargo got hold of the other wrist. He was a lot bigger and a lot stronger and he forced Stubbs back, and twisted.

Stubbs howled in pain and hollered, "Shoot him, Evans, damn you, or we're done for."

Over Stubbs's shoulder, Fargo saw Evans try to take aim. He rammed Stubbs against him and Evans stumbled and nearly dropped the revolver.

Fargo's own six-shooter was wedged under Stubbs's belt. He let go of Stubbs and grabbed for it but Stubbs shifted and slashed. Fargo was forced back. He bumped a broken crate. Lunging, he threw it at Stubbs, whirled, and ran for the end of the alley. His skin prickled with the expectation of taking lead but he wasn't shot at. He glanced back as he went around the corner and saw why.

The crate had knocked Stubbs into Evans and both had gone down. Now they were struggling to their feet.

Fargo stopped and pressed his back to the building. Hiking his leg, he slid his hand under his pants and molded his hand to the Arkansas toothpick. He expected them to come after them.

He coiled, ready to strike, but no one appeared. He didn't hear the slightest sound. His impatience got the better of him and he took a quick peek.

The alley was empty.

"What the hell?"

They had run off. Why, when they had his pistol? Fargo wondered. Maybe they were smarter than he thought they were.

Holding the toothpick against his leg, Fargo jogged along the rear of the buildings until he came to a side street. Turning up it, he went to the street Hauk's Saloon was on. He looked in both directions but Stubbs and Evans were long gone.

Fargo bit down his bubbling fury. He wasn't mad that they'd tried to kill him. He'd always figured they might. No, he was mad that they took his Colt. He wanted it back, and by God, he would get it.

Replacing the toothpick in his ankle sheath, Fargo headed for the Floyd farm. The pair were bound to figure he would come after them so he had to be careful. He checked behind him every block or so and avoided dark patches.

A single window glowed in the farmhouse. The barn was dark and quiet. So were the rows of tents.

Fargo crept toward his. He'd arm himself with his Henry and search the whole property. He pushed on the flap and poked his head in—and his skull seemed to cave in on itself.

40

A cool sensation brought Fargo out of a black pit. He opened his eyes and wished he hadn't. Pain spiked down to his toes. Something was in his mouth. He tried to spit it out and couldn't; it was a gag. He tried to take the gag out but his arms wouldn't move. Neither would his legs. He raised his head and discovered he had been tied to fence rails with his arms and legs outspread. It had to be Stubbs's and Evans's doing, but he couldn't fathom why.

A huge shape materialized out of the darkness.

Fargo caught a pungent odor and heard a grunt. Then he realized. He was in the corral. And so was Myrtle. Texas Jack had been putting her in a stall in the barn at night. A stall with a trough filled with mash and whiskey so that every drink she took kept her peaceful.

Behind him, on the other side of the rails, safe on the outside, someone chortled.

"You're awake," Stubbs said.

Fargo swore through the gag.

"You're probably wondering why you're still alive. I was going to tie you and cut on you some but then I had a better idea. Would you like to hear it?"

"Go to hell," Fargo said. It came out as "Guh ta ell."

"I don't want blame pointed at me. But that buff, there. Everyone will think she got out of her stall and came through the barn to the corral and you were in here and she killed you. Pretty clever, huh?"

Fargo saw that Myrtle was staring at him. Or was she listening to Stubbs?

"In a minute I'm going to prod her into killing you. When

she's done, I'll cut the ropes so no one will ever know you were tied when you died."

Fargo pulled and strained.

"Struggle all you want. I tie good knots. You won't get free."

Fargo twisted his head. The light in the farmhouse was out. Everyone at the farm was asleep.

"Forget it." Stubbs guessed what he was thinking. "There's no one to help."

Fargo tried to twist his wrists.

"How to goad the buff into goring you, that was the problem," Stubbs babbled on. "Then I saw this poking out of the hay."

Something brushed Fargo's shoulder. A long handle was being slid between the rails. At the end of it were four long metal tines.

"That's right," Stubbs said. "A pitchfork. What do you reckon will happen when I jab the buffalo?"

Myrtle was close enough. She was staring at Fargo as if she couldn't quite figure out what he was or why he was stuck to the fence.

"Adios, bastard," Stubbs said, and drove the tines into her high on her front leg.

Fargo tensed. He imagined her huge head ramming into him, imagined her horns impaling him and ripping his innards out.

Myrtle stared at the pitchfork—and didn't move.

"What the hell?" Stubbs said. He drew the pitchfork back and speared her again.

Myrtle swished her tail.

"Goddamn it. She's so damn dumb, she can't tell I'm stabbing her."

Fargo couldn't help himself. He laughed.

"Make a jackass out of me, will she?" Stubbs said. "We'll see about that."

The pitchfork was withdrawn. A hand gripped the rail and Stubbs climbed over. He hesitated, eyeing Myrtle, unsure if it was safe.

Fargo was hoping someone in the tents would hear his voice and come to investigate.

"I wouldn't have to go to all this bother if that bastard Evans hadn't run out on me. He didn't want any part of a killing."

Shows which one of you has brains, Fargo wanted to say but couldn't because of the gag.

"Yellow son of a bitch. Wait until I see him again."

Myrtle was licking her leg.

"I'm not yellow, though," Stubbs said. "I do what needs doing." Squaring his shoulders, he edged around behind Myrtle. She was so busy licking, she paid him no mind.

Fargo bucked against the ropes.

"That's it," Stubbs said. "Waste yourself. Feel how hopeless it is."

Fargo would have given anything to be able to kill him with his bare hands.

"You have less than a minute to live," Stubbs crowed. Gripping the pitchfork, he raised it over his head. "Any last words? What's that? I can't hear you." He laughed at his little joke.

Myrtle stopped licking.

"I hope she rips your guts out," Stubbs said, and stabbed her in the rump.

41

Fargo braced for the concussion of the buffalo's head smashing into him. She'd shatter every rib and his backbone, besides.

Stubbs jerked the tines out and peered around her. "What the hell? Why isn't she killing you?"

Myrtle just stood there.

"You stupid buff. If that didn't do the job, maybe this will." Stubbs drove the tines into her backside, not once, not twice, but three times. At the third, Myrtle uttered a loud snort, lowered her head, and dug at the ground with a front hoof.

"At last," Stubbs said.

For all their bulk, buffalo could wheel on the head of a coin when they wanted to—and Myrtle wanted to. She spun and was on Stubbs before he could blink. Her head caught him full in the chest and he was lifted off his feet and flung against the rails. Stunned, he slumped to the ground.

Myrtle snorted and pawed, and charged.

Stubbs scrambled to his feet, or tried to. He was halfway up when she hooked a horn that caught him low in his thigh. A wrench of her powerful neck, and she ripped him open clear to his groin.

Stubbs screamed. The buffalo pulled away and he fell and sought to crawl off.

Myrtle wasn't done. She pinned him with her head and raked one horn and then the other across his torso.

A ghastly shriek was torn from Stubbs's throat.

Myrtle drove a horn into his abdomen. When she pulled it out, intestines dangled from the tip. She took a step back and drove at him again.

Stubbs's ribs shattered and cracked like kindling. He

screeched and blubbered and looked over at Fargo in incredulity, and went limp.

Myrtle stopped goring him. She fixed her gaze on Fargo.

He held himself still, thinking this was it. Her eyes glittered in the starlight like dark coals as she came up and touched her nose to his buckskin shirt.

Fargo broke out in a sweat.

Myrtle sniffed. She lowered her head and snorted. She dug at the ground, then raised her head and licked him on the chin and went on licking.

By then men were shouting and people were running from the tents and others from the farmhouse. Lantern light washed over the corral. A stunned silence fell, broken when someone said, "Shouldn't we do something?"

Calhoun and Lefty climbed on the fence on either side of Fargo. Knives flashed, and his wrists were free.

Myrtle was still licking him.

"Got yourself a new gal, do you, pard?" the Texan drily asked.

"I see what you mean about him having a way with the ladies," Lefty remarked. "But he sure picks ugly ones."

Fargo rubbed his wrists as they cut the ropes around his ankles. Myrtle had finally stopped licking and was tranquilly gazing at all those lining the rails. Fargo patted her and she rubbed against his palm.

"Yep," Lefty said, "she's sweet on you."

An hour later Fargo was at the kitchen table in the farmhouse sipping his third cup of coffee. Texas Jack sat across from him and Councilman Floyd was to his left.

A Captain Patterson from the Saint Louis Police Department was pacing. His men were out at the corral preparing to cart the body off. "I don't like this," Patterson said. A big slab of a man, his uniform was impeccable, his mustache neatly clipped. "I don't like this at all, Councilman. That animal is a menace and should be put down."

"Menace, hell," Fargo said, and touched a spot of dry buffalo slobber on his cheek.

"It's killed a man," Captain Patterson said.

Texas Jack fished his flask out. "You heard why. Poor Myrtle was provoked."

"I understand that," Captain Patterson said, "but once an animal has killed it will kill again."

"Bullshit," Fargo said.

"I beg your pardon."

"When a bear gets the taste of human flesh that holds true sometimes," Fargo said. "The same with a mountain lion. But buffalo don't kill without cause. And Myrtle sure as hell had cause."

"I don't much care for your tone, sir," Captain Patterson said.

"I don't much care what you don't much care for."

"Gentlemen, please," Councilman Floyd interceded. "We've been arguing about this for how long now?" He looked at the policeman. "Frank, be reasonable. Yes, the buffalo attacked that man but only after he repeatedly stabbed her with a pitchfork. Any of the cows I used to own would have done the same. It hardly makes the buffalo a man-killer."

"If a dog attacks anyone we put it down," Captain Patterson said.

"A buffalo is a far cry from a dog," Councilman Floyd said. "This is an exceptional case with extraordinary circumstances. Surely the department can bend its rules this once?"

"I shouldn't. It will be my head on the block if there's another incident." Patterson sighed and stopped pacing.

"As a personal favor?"

"Since it's you I'll do it," Captain Patterson said. He stepped to the table and glared at Texas Jack. "But understand this, Mr. Lavender. Should that beast of yours so much as nick someone with a horn or step on a bystander's foot, my men will shoot her and have her slaughtered for the butcher. Do I make myself clear?"

Texas Jack chugged and smiled and raised the flask in a salute. "Perfectly. Don't worry, though. You have my word that the rest of our stay in your fair city will go as smooth as a tart's bottom."

"Oh, Jack," Councilman Floyd said.

"I sincerely hope it does," Captain Patterson said. "But I'll be honest with you. I very much doubt it will."

Fargo didn't come out and say it, but so did he.

42

The great day arrived.

Texas Jack was in new finery. His buckskins had whangs half a foot long and were decorated with enough red and blue beads to cover a buckboard. His ivory-handled revolvers were around his waist and his silver flask was prominent in his shirt pocket.

Fargo was at the corral, watching Calhoun and Lefty feed Myrtle more whiskey-soaked mash so she wouldn't misbehave during her performance when Texas Jack sauntered over, all smiles and reeking.

"I tell you, Skye, this is the day I've lived all my life for. The day when the name of Texas Jack Lavender becomes as famous as Daniel Boone or Kit Carson."

"You don't say."

Jack leaned on the rails. "I need your advice."

"Put the flask in your back pocket."

"Eh? Not about that. I need advice on what to call the show."

"Texas Jack's Folly sounds good to me," Fargo said.

"Can't you ever be serious? I've been billing it as the Great Frontier Extravaganza Starring Real Scouts of the Plains Complete with Raging Buffalo and Red Devils."

"I remember."

"But we only have the one buffalo, and she's so soused now, she wouldn't rage if we beat her with a shovel. As for the red devils, we have High Eagle and that old toothless Otoe I found at a saloon."

"There's Tiberius."

"He's so cute and cuddly, he's not likely to inspire much awe." Texas Jack chewed his lower lip. "No, I'm thinking of calling it the Great Frontier Extravaganza Starring the Greatest Scout Who Ever Lived. Namely, me. What do you think?"

"Very humble," Fargo said.

"I know. I admit that's one of my few failings. But how can I be humble when I see my reflection in the mirror every day?"

"There's that," Fargo said.

"It's a trial being me. But at last I can let my greatness out for all the world to see."

"Do you think the world is ready?"

"Let's find out."

The stands were filled and people were four to five deep along the arena fence. Four musicians, at a signal from Texas Jack, launched into a brass rendition of "The Star-Spangled Banner." As the music reached a crescendo, Texas Jack entered the arena astride a white stallion. He rose in the stirrups and waved and smiled.

The crowd went wild.

From his vantage on the top rail of the corral, Fargo could see it all. He was in his best buckskins but they were nowhere near as grand as Jack's. About twenty minutes into the production, Jack would introduce him and he was to put on a short shooting display.

"He sure is a spectacle," Calhoun said on the rail to his right.

"About the prettiest man I ever did see," Lefty agreed on the left, and cackled.

"I couldn't do that," Calhoun said. "I can't stand to have folks starin' at me."

"I could do it if I was drunk enough," Lefty said.

"Maybe that's his secret."

Fargo grinned. As long as he had known Jack, Jack had always been . . . What was that word? Flamboyant. "When do you two take Myrtle in?"

"Not until you're done shootin'," Calhoun said.

"We should probably see to gettin' her ready," Lefty said. "Give the gal a little more mash so she can't hardly think straight."

"Thank God Jack changed his mind about the stockin's," Calhoun remarked.

"Stockings?" Fargo said.

Lefty nodded. "Last night Jack got this notion to put stockings over her horns. Long pink ones, like the ladies wear. But then he figured no, he wanted her to look dangerous."

"That's our Jack," Calhoun said.

They hopped down and went into the barn.

Fargo listened to Jack go on about the perils of the plains. How Jack once fought off a band of Comanches to save a wagon train. How Jack killed a Sioux chief to save a captured white woman. How Jack rode two hundred miles in one night to bring relief to a cavalry patrol beset by a horde of Blackfeet. On and on Jack went, and not a lick of it was true.

Fargo jumped down and took his gun belt from his saddlebag and strapped it on. The police had given permission for the performers to wear their sidearms for the show. He climbed on the Ovaro and rode around to the gate into the arena. A lot of the company were there. The old Otoe too, so wrinkled and leathery his skin looked like parchment.

Reese came up. "Have you seen any sign of that damn Pawnee?"

Fargo shook his head.

"He was supposed to be here by now. Him and that gal, both. Where can they have gotten to?"

Fargo had no time to answer.

Texas Jack was introducing him.

43

"Here he is, ladies and gentlemen. The genuine article if ever there was one. The marksman who took part in the famous Springfield sharpshooting contest with Dottie Wheatridge and Buck Smith. The man some have taken to calling the Trailsman. I give you the one and only Skye Fargo."

A thunderous ovation rose as Fargo rode into the arena. He did as Jack wanted and made a circuit waving and smiling. Drawing rein, he shucked the Henry and alighted.

"Listen to them," Jack said as the people went on cheering and clapping. "I eat this up like honey."

Not Fargo. He felt a bit of a fool putting himself on display. Then and there he came to a decision. Continuing to smile and wave, he said, "This is the last one of these I'll do."

"What?"

"You like this. I don't. I'd rather have a tooth pulled."

"You're still going to shoot for me today?" Jack asked, sounding worried.

"I said I would."

Local boys that Jack had hired were setting up the targets. Plates were hung from poles. Melons were lined up on a bench.

A bull's-eye was set up a hundred yards out.

"Now then, all of you fine people," Texas Jack regaled them. "My good friend, the man whose life I saved from a rampaging grizzly, the man who once said he would do anything for me and all I had to do was ask—"

"Go to hell, Jack," Fargo said quietly. "This is the first and last and that's final."

"—the man whose word is his bond, who would never turn his back on a friend in need, a plainsman with the eyes of a hawk and nerves of iron, will demonstrate why he is feared across this great land by evildoers everywhere."

"You're laying it on a little thick, aren't you?"

"Behold and be dazzled by the only shooter alive who the great Dottie Wheatridge said is her equal." Jack smiled and said out of the corner of his mouth, "I'm done."

"Thank God."

Fargo faced the poles. The plates were hanging from cords that the boys set to swinging and then moved out of harm's way. Raising the Henry, he took aim. In swift succession, methodically working the lever, he broke the first, the second, the third, and the fourth. The range was only twenty yards and the plates were full-sized supper plates. To him it was no feat at all but the stands and the people around the fence offered more applause.

"Tell me you don't love that," Texas Jack said. "Tell me you couldn't grow used to it."

Fargo moved so he was in a line with the table. The six melons had been set on end. He upended or split each with blast after blast.

Once again the crowd responded enthusiastically.

Fargo felt like he was cheating them, the shots were so easy. "You should have used apples."

"The next time I will."

"You're not listening. There's not going to be a next time."

"I can't hear you."

"How about if I shoot you instead of the target?"

"You're quite the joker." Texas Jack raised his arms and turned. "And now, ladies and gentlemen, your indulgence, if you please. I must ask for complete silence. For you see, it's not enough that my good friend will hit the last target. No, he is going to hit it in the exact dead center."

Fargo reloaded. He finished and took a bead on the bull's-eye. He held his breath and started to curl his finger around the trigger.

"How about a wager?" Texas Jack said.

Fargo paused, his concentration spoiled. "How much?"

"Not for money. For you." Jack grinned. "If you're off, if you miss by so much as a hair, you agree to stay with my Extravaganza until the end of our Eastern tour."

"You never give up, do you?"

"What do you say?"

"No." Fargo aligned the front sight with the rear sight and willed himself to relax.

"You're worse than my grandmother. She never took chances, either, and ended her days a lonely widow in a rocking chair."

Fargo didn't see what that had to do with anything. He paid no more mind to Jack, his whole attention fixed on the target. When he was sure beyond any shadow of a doubt, he stroked the trigger. The Henry boomed and bucked.

Down the arena a boy ran to the target and touched a finger to the center to show where the slug penetrated.

"Dead center!" he shouted.

The people cheered louder than ever.

"You have plenty of time to change your mind," Jack told him.

Fargo waved and bowed and was glad to get out of there.

Calhoun and Lefty were at the gate with Myrtle, waiting their turn to go in.

"You did right fine," Calhoun complimented him.

"You're a natural," Lefty agreed. "You should do it for a living."

"I'd as soon gut myself," Fargo said, and rode around to the corral. He climbed down, tied the reins, and was about to climb to the top rail to watch the buffalo act when he happened to glance at the ticket shack at the side of the stands. High Eagle and Mandy were just coming out.

High Eagle had a rifle.

Mandy was holding a bulging burlap sack.

44

They were around the shack and into the crowd when Fargo reached it. The door was partway open and he heard a muffled sound from inside. A quick look revealed the four women Texas Jack had hired to sell tickets and collect money were bound and gagged. So was the guard, an off-duty policeman in uniform. The man was unconscious and blood was trickling from a gash in his head.

Fargo went after them. He had left the Henry in the scabbard but he was still wearing the Colt. His hand on the grips, he shouldered into the press of onlookers along the arena fence. The pair couldn't have gotten far. He wasn't looking to hurt them. With luck he could get the drop on them and persuade Mandy to return the money. A judge might let them off easy if they did it of their own accord.

Out in the arena, Texas Jack was playing to his audience.

"And now, ladies and gentlemen, boys and girls, you are about to behold a beastly wonder. All of you have no doubt heard of the formidable lords of the plains, the fierce buffalo that roam in mighty herds of a million strong. But how many of you have ever seen one? How many of you have stood close to one of these magnificent brutes? How many of you have looked one in the eye, as I have done, and tamed them by the force of your will?"

The crowed hung on every word.

"Get set, then. For you are to be treated to a sight few have seen. Only those intrepid souls who have ventured into the forbidding West have beheld what you are about to behold. I give you an engine of destruction. I give you a living, breathing buffalo."

That was the cue for Calhoun and Lefty to bring Myrtle

in. They had ropes around her neck and one rode on either side. She came peacefully enough until the throng erupted with applause. Suddenly stopping, Myrtle tossed her head in annoyance.

Fargo caught it all as he scanned the press for Mandy and High Eagle. He thought he glimpsed the back of Mandy's head. A man hawking sweet cakes blocked his view and he pushed him aside.

"Hey, what's the idea, mister?"

Fargo swore. Mandy was gone. He threaded through a cluster of men in overalls and straw hats. Again he caught sight of her; she was nervously glancing around. He went faster.

"As you can see," Texas Jack was shouting, "buffalo live up to their reputations. Their size alone is enough to make grown men cringe. Note, too, the sweep of those sharp horns, and the hooves that can pound a person to a pulp."

Fargo was thinking that maybe Mandy and High Eagle had cut across to lose themselves in the city when he saw the Pawnee moving through the onlookers below the bottom row on the stands.

Mandy was a few paces behind him.

Out in the arena, Calhoun and Lefty had slipped their ropes off Myrtle and were returning to the gate.

Myrtle appeared confused by the commotion, or by Texas Jack, who was slowly moving toward her.

"Watch, now, as I do what no human being has ever done. I am going to walk up to this monster and pat it on the head. And then you will be treated to a display that will dazzle one and all. You will witness an historic moment when a young Indian climbs on this beast and rides it."

Fargo was almost to the stands.

Mandy looked back and saw him and stopped. She said something to High Eagle. The Pawnee turned. Without any warning or hesitation, he jerked the rifle to his shoulder and fired.

Fargo dived for the ground. Above him a man grunted and a woman screamed and wet drops spattered Fargo's cheek. He pushed up, drew his Colt.

High Eagle's rifle cracked a second time.

The forehead of a woman Fargo was passing showered

flesh and bone. He raised the Colt but several people got in the way.

A man lunged at High Eagle and the warrior shot him through the chest.

Panic erupted. Shouts and screams filled the air.

Anyone near the Pawnee sought to get somewhere else.

Mandy grabbed High Eagle's arm and yelled but Fargo couldn't hear her over the bedlam.

Texas Jack had stopped his oration and was facing the stands. "What's going on over there? What's all the shooting about?"

High Eagle pushed Mandy's hand off. Turning, he brought his rifle to bear and shot Texas Jack.

45

It happened so fast, there was nothing Fargo could do. Again he tried to put a slug into High Eagle and again panicked people got in his way.

High Eagle ran in the other direction, pulling Mandy after him.

A policeman rushed out of the swarm, brandishing his nightstick. High Eagle shot him in the face. A man in a suit tried to grab the rifle and High Eagle smashed the stock against his chin and when the man folded, shot him in the back of the head.

Fargo swore. He couldn't get a clear shot.

More police were converging, descending from up in the stands and from the vicinity of the gate.

High Eagle stopped. He looked both ways and over his shoulder at Fargo. Knocking a woman and her child aside, he turned to the fence. A lithe leap and his outstretched hand gripped the top. He was up and over before Fargo could shoot. He shouted at Mandy and gestured and she tossed the burlap bag over. She jumped and caught hold. With an effort she managed to hook one leg over. From there it was easy to swing to the other side and join High Eagle in a race for the far side of the arena.

"Out of the way!" Fargo bellowed. Shoving the Colt into his holster, he ran to fence. He sprang and pulled and was on the other side.

High Eagle and Mandy were out near the middle. Mandy was falling behind but High Eagle either hadn't noticed or didn't care.

Fargo gave chase. He saw Texas Jack sprawled in the dirt

and a spreading crescent of red blood, and molten fire filled his veins.

High Eagle stopped and spun. He dropped the burlap bag and raised his Spencer. Mandy moved in front of the barrel and he knocked her down. Quick as lightning, he squeezed off a shot.

Fargo dived again. A hornet buzzed him and he was up and running. He didn't shoot. Mandy had risen and was trying to wrest the rifle from High Eagle. The Pawnee tore loose and smashed the barrel against her ear and she crumpled. He took aim.

At last Fargo had a clear shot. He extended the Colt, thumbed back the hammer.

Out of nowhere hurtled a massive mountain of hair and muscle. High Eagle must have caught sight of the buffalo out of the corner of his eye because he whirled a split instant before Myrtle slammed into him. Her horns missed his body and somehow he got his arms around them so that when she tried to toss him, she couldn't. High Eagle clung like glue, his rifle gone, scarlet spurting from his nose from the impact to his chest.

Mandy screamed.

Fargo had twenty yards to cover to reach her. He shouted her name but she ran after the buffalo.

Myrtle stopped and shook her head to dislodge High Eagle. He slipped but didn't fall. Wheeling, she galloped the other way. Once more she stopped and sought to shake him off.

A lot of the audience had stopped to gape.

Calhoun and Lefty came through the gate on their horses, flying to help.

Myrtle bucked and plunged. Suddenly she flew toward the fence, High Eagle clinging tight. Once he let go he was as good as dead.

Mandy sprinted after them, and Fargo put all he had into overtaking her. He called to her but he was wasting his breath.

Myrtle was moving as fast as any buffalo could, thirty to forty miles an hour. She slowed as she neared the fence and Fargo couldn't figure out what she was up to until he realized she wasn't going to stop.

At the last moment High Eagle realized the same thing.

He attempted to push clear but he never made it. Myrtle rammed into the fence with him on her head. The impact burst his torso like a cantaloupe and his innards and copious amounts of blood rained down. That wasn't enough for Myrtle. She smashed him against the fence two more times. When she stopped and stepped back, what was left of High Eagle's body oozed to the earth like so much mangled wax.

Mandy was screaming her head off. She ran up to Myrtle and punched her near her tail.

"Noooooo!" Fargo bawled.

Myrtle spun. Whether she intended to or not, her horn hooked into Mandy where Mandy's legs met her body. Mandy was swept off her feet and hung suspended in the air.

Cries of horror rose. Children wailed in terror.

Fargo reached Myrtle. She stood there staring at him, blood and gore dripping from her muzzle. "You poor buff," he said. He holstered his Colt, grasped Mandy's arms, and eased her off the horn. He would never forget the squishing sound.

More blood and some of Mandy's insides spilled out as he gently lowered her onto her back. He said to Myrtle, "They'll kill you for this."

Myrtle licked him.

"It wasn't her fault," Mandy said in less than a whisper.

Fargo looked down.

"It was mine." Mandy was pale and shaking and sounds were coming from the cavity below her waist.

"I know."

"Don't hate me."

"Never."

"I don't know what got into me. We wanted money. Lots and lots of money."

Fargo clasped her hand and her nails dug into his skin. "Stay still. A doctor is bound to come."

"It won't do any good. I'll see my ma and pa sooner than I reckoned."

"Damn you," Fargo said.

"Did you see him take the sack and run? All he cared about was the money. I was such a fool." Mandy gripped him harder. "A last request. I don't have any kin."

"I'll see to the grave."

"Thank you." Mandy smiled through the blood. "You've been so—"

Fargo would never hear the rest. He closed her eyes and bowed his head.

46

The newspapers called it "the first-ever buffalo execution."
It was to take place in three days. Councilman Floyd and
other politicians were to attend and give speeches before the
"killer buffalo" was put down.

The police took charge of Myrtle. She was kept under guard
in the corral at the Floyd farm.

Fargo was in Haut's Saloon, halfway through a bottle,
when the batwings opened and in came Calhoun and Lefty.
They strolled over and claimed chairs, Calhoun turning his
and straddling it.

"Figured we'd find you here."

Fargo filled his glass and raised it aloft. "To Texas Jack,"
he toasted.

"The jackass," Lefty said.

"It's not his fault he was shot," Calhoun said.

"It's a shame he'll live," Lefty said. "At least that shoulder
wound will lay him up for a couple of weeks."

"Deep down Jack is all right," Calhoun said.

"Deep down Jack is so full of himself, it leaks out his ears."

"Gents," Fargo said. "I didn't ask you here to talk about him."

"Myrtle," Calhoun said.

"It ain't fair," Lefty said. "It ain't fair and it ain't right.
You can't blame a buffalo for being a buffalo."

"No," Fargo agreed. "You can't."

Calhoun said, "They've got six or seven guards around
the corral twenty-four hours a day."

Lefty snorted. "I was over there earlier. Those city boys
are so scared of her, they'd faint if she farted."

"What can we do?" Calhoun asked, looking at Fargo.

"We save her."

"How, exactly?"

"We sneak her out of the city and let her loose on the prairie."

Calhoun's eyebrows tried to climb into his hair. "Sneak—a buffalo?"

Fargo nodded.

"Maybe you noticed she's bigger than a breadbasket? It's not as if we can stick her in our pocket."

"She's temperamental, to boot," Lefty said. "If those police ain't keepin' her soused, she's liable to gore us for tryin' to help."

"If she's not soused we souse her," Fargo said. "Are you with me or not?"

"Count me in," Lefty said without hesitation.

"I'm for it," Calhoun said, "but I'd rather not be thrown in jail."

Fargo glanced at the clock above the bar. "It's eleven twenty. At midnight we'll head over."

"It's a shame about that gal," Lefty said. "I liked her. She was always sweet as sugar."

Fargo drained his glass.

"That fool Pawnee," Lefty said. "What was he thinkin'? What do Injuns need with money, anyhow?"

"Enough about them," Fargo said gruffly.

The minute hand made its slow sweep. When both hands were straight up, Fargo rose and went to the bar. He paid for two bottles and brought them back.

"Ready?"

Calhoun rose. "They catch us, they'll want our hides."

"And Myrtle's," Lefty said.

Not many people were abroad at that time of night and hardly any at all the closer they came to the farm.

Fargo drew rein a few hundred yards from the barn and strapped on his Colt.

"We're not goin' to shoot them, are we?" Calhoun asked as he strapped on his.

"No shooting. No killing."

"Shucks," Lefty said.

They rode closer and dismounted on the far side of the farmhouse. The house was dark. A lantern glowed in the barn and another hung on a nail driven into the top rail of the corral. Two policemen were bathed in its glow, talking.

"The rest must be in the barn," Lefty whispered.

"There's one," Fargo said, pointing

Almost invisible in the dark, another policeman was walking around the corral.

"You'd think they're afraid that buff will break out and escape," Calhoun said.

Oblivious to the police and her impending fate, Myrtle peacefully dozed.

"We'll take the ones in the barn first," Fargo said, and glided toward it. The wide door was open enough for him to slip quietly in.

Three more police were at the other end. A table and chairs had been set up near the back door and they were drinking coffee and playing cards.

Fargo had to be careful. The last thing he wanted was to spill their blood. They were only doing their jobs.

A dark-haired policeman was doing most of the talking.

"—buy a few pounds of the meat my own self. Did you see what that thing did to her? Horrible, it was."

"I was there, remember?" another said. "It'll give me nightmares the rest of my days."

"I hear the town council is going to pass an ordinance against buffalo in the city limits."

"Leave it to the politicians," the last man said. "They're always a day late and a brain short."

That brought laughter that was cut off when Fargo and his companions rose out of the shadows with their revolvers leveled.

"Call out and you're dead," Fargo bluffed. "I want each of you to get up, nice and slow, and lie on the ground with your hands behind your backs."

"The devil we will," the dark-haired policeman said.

"If'n you don't, city boy," Lefty said, patting his knife, "it'll take a month of Sundays to stitch the pieces back together."

Tying and gagging them took longer than Fargo liked.

Calhoun stood watch at the door.

All three of the policemen outside were in the ring of light.

"They'll see us the moment we step out," Calhoun whispered.

"Not if we blow out the lantern in here," Lefty said.

"No," Fargo said. "It would make them suspicious." He went to the bound officers, untied one, and made him remove his coat at gunpoint. After retying the man, he slipped the coat on over his buckskins, gave his hat to Calhoun, and donned the officer's. It was a tight fit.

"Pretty sneaky," Lefty complimented him.

Fargo held the Colt behind him as he ambled out with his head low so his beard wasn't obvious. The police were clean shaven.

"Is it your turn already, Hargrove?" one of the men outside asked.

Stopping, Fargo pointed his Colt. "Hargrove is all tied up."

"What's this?" one said, brandishing his nightstick.

"I wouldn't, mister," Calhoun said, coming at them from the side as Lefty approached from the other. "We don't want to shoot you but we will if you force us."

"Speak for yourself, pard," Lefty said.

Once all the officers were trussed, Fargo sent Lefty to fetch their horses. He and Calhoun filled the corral trough with corn and water.

Myrtle watched with interest.

The lights stayed out in the farmhouse. The night was quiet, save for the barking of dogs and the occasional mew of a cat.

The bottles were in Fargo's saddlebags. He opened them and upended both over the trough. The whiskey gushed down with a *clug-clug*.

Myrtle sniffed. Her tail bobbing, she trotted over and dipped her muzzle in, lapping thirstily.

"Will you look that?" Lefty said. "We've turned her into a drunk."

Ten minutes later the trough was empty and Myrtle was swaying.

"Now," Fargo said.

They climbed on their horses and Calhoun and Lefty uncoiled their ropes. Fargo opened the gate and held it open as they gigged their mounts in. He was half afraid Myrtle would resist but she let them throw their loops and came along as meekly as a calf.

"She's gotten used to this," Calhoun said.

The city limits were nearest south of them. They led Myrtle along dark side streets and across vacant lots and a field. All went well until a dog came running from a house and barked furiously. Lights came on, and a man in a robe opened the front door and stepped outside.

"Here now," he called. "What's all this ruckus at this hour?"

"Ask your damn mongrel," Lefty said quietly.

"What's that you've got there?" the man asked, craning his neck. "What are you doing?"

"It's a cow," Fargo said. "She got out of her pen and we're taking her back."

"Oh. I see. Well, she could have picked a more decent hour, couldn't she?" The man beckoned to the dog. "Come along, Ferdinand. That's a good boy."

The man and his dog went inside.

"Ferdinand?" Calhoun said.

"Some folks are idiots," Lefty said.

Fargo nodded at Myrtle. "Do we have room to talk?"

A quarter of an hour later farmland stretched before them. They turned west along a dirt road and after a few miles the farms dwindled.

They were on open prairie.

"Here?" Calhoun said.

"Not yet." Fargo wouldn't risk having Myrtle stray back into Saint Louis. The police might shoot her on sight. He wasn't satisfied until they had put a few more miles behind them.

On a windswept knoll he drew rein.

"Careful, pard," Calhoun urged, "or you're liable to end up like Mandy."

Working slowly so as not to provoke her, Fargo removed first one rope and then the other from around Myrtle's thick neck. Myrtle didn't move. Not until the ropes were off. Then she sniffed him and ran her sticky tongue across his face and down over his chin.

"If I didn't know better," Lefty said, chuckling, "I'd swear that critter was in love."

Fargo rubbed Myrtle's head and gave her a smack. "Off you go, girl."

Myrtle licked him one more time, grunted, and trotted into the night. The last they saw of her was her bobbing tail.

"And that's that," Lefty said.

Fargo climbed back on the Ovaro.

"Lefty and me have talked it over and we're headin' for Texas," Calhoun revealed. "You're welcome to join us if you'd like."

"Be right honored," Lefty said.

"No, thanks," Fargo told them. "I'll be seeing you around."

He touched his hat brim and tapped his spurs. He'd had his fill of civilization for a while.

The plains and the mountains were calling his name.

LOOKING FORWARD!
The following is the opening section of the next novel in the exciting *Trailsman* series from Signet:

TRAILSMAN #360
TEXAS LEAD SLINGERS

The Gulf coast of Texas, 1861—
where a high-stakes poker tournament
leads to deceit and death.

The two men latched on to Skye Fargo when he stopped at the saloon. He'd been on the trail for three days and wanted to wash the dust down before he went out to the mansion. Over a dozen of the top poker players in the country had been invited to take part in Senator Deerforth's annual high-stakes game, and he was on the list.

The sun had set and lights were coming on the length of Deerforth's main street. Named after the man who invited him, the Gulf town was booming. Silver was the reason: the largest deposit in south Texas.

The bar was three deep. Fargo shouldered through and pounded on it to get the barkeep's attention. He hankered after a bottle but settled for a glass. Wiping his mouth with the sleeve of his buckskin shirt, he sauntered back out and was unwrapping the Ovaro's reins from the hitch rail when he became aware of a pair of hard-eyed men who were leaning against the wall. Their clothes marked them as sailors.

Fargo didn't think much of it and led the stallion down Main Street. When he glanced back the pair was following him. They tried not to be obvious but they might as well wear signs.

He didn't know what to make of it.

The next junction was Cutter Street. He turned right. Cutter ran down to the docks. A schooner was out on the water, raising sail. Other ships were at anchor, some being loaded, others unloaded.

Fargo made for a broad patch of shadow cast by a clipper. A lantern glowed on board but no one was moving about. Letting the reins drop, he crouched and circled to a stack of crates.

The pair stopped and gazed out to sea. The tallest scratched under an arm and sniffed his fingers. The other fingered the hilt of a knife. They kept glancing at the Ovaro.

"What's he doing, Ranson?" asked the man with the knife. He had a chin that came to a point, and buck teeth.

"I can't tell much," the tall man replied. "I can see the horse but I can't see him."

"Do we do it or not?"

"We took half in advance, Jules."

"Then let's get it over with."

Ranson slid a dagger from his left sleeve. "We have to be careful. He's supposed to be tough."

"Tough, hell," Jules said. "You distract him and I'll earn us the rest."

"Nice of him to come to the docks," Ranson said. "Not many around at this time of day to notice."

"Damned nice," Jules agreed.

They moved toward the Ovaro.

By then Fargo had his Colt in his hand. He glided from behind the crates and smashed the barrel against Jules's head, pulping Jules's ear and felling him like a shot hog.

Ranson spun, his dagger glinting in the starlight. "What the hell?" he blurted.

Fargo leveled his six-gun and thumbed back the hammer.

"I wouldn't," he warned. "Not unless you want your brains splattered all over your pard."

Ranson straightened and dropped his dagger. "If this is a robbery we don't have much money, mister."

"Who paid you to kill me?"

"I don't know what in hell you're talkin' about," Ranson said.

"I heard you."

"You didn't hear us say nothing about killing. And since when is talk against the law, anyhow?"

"Do you see a badge?" Fargo said.

"If you were you might have some excuse for this but since you're not, you must be a footpad."

"The bluff won't wash."

"Then take us to the marshal and we'll see what he has to say."

Fargo had no proof the pair were plotting to assassinate him. It'd be their word against his.

"Well?" Ranson prodded.

Fargo could have shot them but one was unconscious and the other was unarmed.

"Are you going to stand there pointing that thing at me all night?"

"No," Fargo said, and slammed the Colt against Ranson's temple. The tall sailor joined his companion in a sprawled heap.

Twirling the Colt into his holster, Fargo climbed on the Ovaro. He hoped he wasn't making a mistake leaving these two alive.

Time would tell.

No other series packs this much heat!

THE TRAILSMAN

Follow the trail of Penguin's Action Westerns at
penguin.com/actionwesterns   S310

National Bestselling Author

RALPH COMPTON

GRITTY WESTERN ACTION FROM

USA TODAY BESTSELLING AUTHOR

RALPH
COTTON

Available wherever books are sold or at
penguin.com